THE PATH OF MOST RESISTANCE

Also by Russell Wangersky

Walt
Whirl Away (Stories)
The Glass Harmonica
Burning Down the House (Memoir)
The House of Bad Decisions (Stories)

THE PATH OF MOST RESISTANCE

STORIES

RUSSELL WANGERSKY

Published in Canada in 2016 by House of Anansi Press Inc.
www.houseofanansi.com

House of Anansi Press is committed to protecting our natural environment.
As part of our efforts, the interior of this book isprinted on paper that contains
100% post-consumer recycled fibres, is acid-free, and is processed chlorine-free.

20 19 18 17 16   1 2 3 4 5

Library and Archives Canada Cataloguing in Publication

Wangersky, Russell, 1962–, author
The path of most resistance / Russell Wangersky.

Short stories.
Issued in print and electronic formats.
ISBN 978-1-4870-0068-4 (paperback).—ISBN 978-1-4870-0069-1 (html)

I. Title.

PS8645.A5333P38 2016   C813'.6   C2016-900848-7
                                C2016-900849-5

Cover design: Alysia Shewchuk
Typesetting: Erin Mallory
Cover image: Steven Puetzer / Getty Images

 Canada Council   Conseil des Arts
for the Arts   du Canada

ONTARIO ARTS COUNCIL
CONSEIL DES ARTS DE L'ONTARIO
an Ontario government agency
un organisme du gouvernement de l'Ontario

*We acknowledge for their financial support of our publishing program
the Canada Council for the Arts, the Ontario Arts Council, and the Government of
Canada through the Canada Book Fund.*

Printed and bound in Canada

MIX
Paper from
responsible sources
FSC® C004071

For those who fight the hardest to win the smallest of battles. You know who you are.

CONTENTS

THE PATH OF MOST
RESISTANCE

RAGE

IAN WAS RETURNING FROM his doctor's office when he saw the first angry driver at the corner of Belvedere and Circular Road, where the road takes a flat, shallow curve to the left and Circular Road just gives up and stops.

The woman was in the front seat of a burgundy SUV, one of those big cars that Ian thought had a way of pushing the driver up behind the wheel, surveying the rabble in front of them. Ian watched her at the stop sign as he drove closer, sure that she was going to dart out in front of him, ignoring the stop. He was good at anticipating the drivers who swerved suddenly without using their turn signals, good at being ready to brake for the ones who slowed enough at stop signs for you to believe they were stopping before they took the foolish chance and darted out into a space in traffic too narrow for their cars to fit.

Ian was watching her face to see if she'd seen him. He would regularly tell his friends that he thought his car was the colour "invisible" because so many drivers seemed oblivious to him when they turned or stopped or started.

It was late August by then and all the greens in the city had already gone dusty and flat, except for the ones that had already given up and headed toward brown or yellow. Everything appeared in the kind of colours that intuitively tell you that, no matter how hot it still is, the summer is really over. And it had been a hot one, the kind of summer that people would use as a measuring stick for years to come: "It's still not as hot as the summer we had four years ago..." There had been very little rain, but the nights were cool, as if the open, cloudless skies at night let the rooftops and the ground simply throw the heat of the day back out into space.

Ian was thinking about all of that as his car swung into the turn onto Belvedere, just before he glanced over at the woman in the still-stopped car and saw that she was angry. Very angry. She glared at him, clearly mad enough that she wanted him to know and didn't care what he thought about it.

Why is she mad at me? That was Ian's first thought, and he couldn't help but play back the last few seconds in his memory to see if there was something that he had done. Had he touched the brakes, slowing in the way that suggests to another driver that they've been offered some dangerous courtesy? Had his turn signal stayed on after turning onto Belvedere? Was he going too fast? He couldn't think of anything he'd done that would have put him at fault.

He looked in the rear-view mirror and was relieved to see the woman turn the other way, even though she hadn't been signalling a left turn. After seeing her face, Ian hadn't wanted her to be behind him, didn't want that anger tucked right up behind his bumper, tight and tailgating and fuming.

Ian was sure that most accidents happened because of drivers just like her, people who turned their cars around too fast or hugged your bumper too tight, like pressurized containers ready to let loose after the tiniest tap of a rear-ender. Some people, he thought, drive cars like their vehicles are instruments of their emotions, a great steel-and-glass-and-plastic piece of their psyches reaching out onto the road. You can get away with that for a while, Ian thought, then one day you call it too close, trust brakes and traction too much, and everyone's supposed to treat the inevitable as if it was an accident. Accident—he thought about the word, about how so many people applied it to things that weren't accidental at all. An accident is supposed to happen by chance, not at the conclusion of a long, but eminently solvable, equation.

Ian was returning from his annual checkup at the doctor. Dr. Antle had held both of Ian's arms loosely in his grip, like there was something on them that he didn't want to touch, even with the protection of gloves.

Dr. Antle looked at the brown, tanned skin on Ian's left arm, pointed to three little jagged islands of mole, and said just one word — "melanoma" — and of course Ian knew exactly what that meant. Dr. Antle said "dermatologist" and "prognosis" and "serious," but Ian had stopped listening after that first heavy word.

Afterwards, Ian sat in the front seat of his car with the window down and looked at the way his elbow stuck out the window on the driver's side, like it always did, like it was designed to rest right there. Then he pulled his arm back in the window and held it up close to his eyes so that he could focus his vision in tight on the brown skin, on the fine, long hairs that poked up and fell over, all leaning in the same direction like trees bent by a prevailing and constant wind. Ian looked at the plane of his skin with its thousands of small careful interlocking wrinkles and at the patches that had so concerned Dr. Antle. The three ragged-edged blotches that had been there for as long as he could remember. A little familiar collection of raised spots on his arm, no more frightening than any other bump or mole.

Ian then rolled the window up, determined to keep his arm away from the sun, but as he pulled into traffic and the car warmed, he almost immediately and absent-mindedly rolled the window down again, and settled his arm back into its usual place.

As he drove home—the route laid out in his head without even really thinking about it, Belvedere, then Empire, onto the Crosstown, and then into the west end—his mind cleared itself of everything except for the map in his head.

At the second light on Empire—the one by the all-night drugstore and the housing project—he was the first car in line and all the traffic was stopped, waiting while the green turning arrow flashed.

Ian looked across at the cars stopped at the light, peering at the drivers in each one, trying to decide if they would turn right on the red or try to jump quickly with the green. In a small car to the left, he saw two people, a young couple. Ian realized that they were angrily and carefully not looking at each other, their faces absolutely rigid. The man had dark hair, and his mouth was clenched tightly enough that the jaw muscle stood out like a sharply defined slab on the side of his face. The woman was pushed over against the door, her body language indicating that she'd push her way right out through the side of the car if she could.

When the light changed and their car drove by in front of his, the woman caught Ian staring, and, while he wouldn't have thought it possible a moment earlier, her expression became even darker. Why does everyone seem so angry today, Ian wondered. Everyone was angry except him. Ian couldn't manage angry, despite Dr. Antle's news.

I've always been careful about everything, Ian thought. Careful about letting people know too much about me, careful about my heart and exercise and eating well—a hard thing to do when your job is always being on the road—and careful, always careful, while driving.

Ian had been a pharmaceutical rep for twenty-five years. He had been on the road non-stop with a briefcase of colourful literature and foil-backed bubble-pack samples of new drugs or fancy new formulations of old drugs. He didn't mind the work—didn't even really think about the work—not even when he was driving, and more than anything else, the job was about driving.

He'd already logged thousands of kilometres that summer, long drives that kicked out to the very edge of his territory, buying coffee and the occasional lunch for tired doctors and harried-looking office staff. He was good at his job because he didn't actually try to sell anything.

The doctors he visited spent his entire visit waiting for the start of the sales pitch, for the hard sell, for a push to prescribe the latest wonder drug, the expensive one with just a few barely noticeable side effects. Dry mouth, almost always. Headaches. Vivid dreams. "If you notice any of these symptoms ... call your doctor." The doctors waited for his pitch, so there would be a clear spot when they could stop him and tell him they weren't interested.

But Ian didn't sell. He listened while the doctors talked about their workloads, about difficult patients, about the provincial government's curious intransigence about paying for the services the doctors provided. Ian left samples, answered any questions, and then he got in his car and drove away, leaving the pleased, but mystified, physicians behind. Doctors were the same everywhere, Ian thought, they all had too many patients and too little time, expected to listen to every little thing, and packed tight with everybody else's problems. Never able to talk about themselves.

Sometimes he looked at his sales numbers at the end of the month—sales numbers that were remarkably high compared to the other staff in his division—and wondered if some small part of the high totals was a guilty sort of medicinal thank-you, as if the doctors were paying him back for his time, the time he spent quietly listening, silently waiting to get back on the road.

One June afternoon, a doctor in Burgeo had even asked him to come home for dinner with his family. Ian had gone, following the path of least resistance more than anything else, but he thought about it later and wondered if any other reps had ever experienced the same thing. He asked himself if any other rep would even have considered the invitation. Or if the doctor would even have extended it to a different salesman.

Dinner was in a small square light blue house up over the ocean. It was just Ian, the doctor, his wife, and a small daughter. Ian noticed that every single time the daughter needed something, it was the doctor's wife, Anne, who got up from her chair.

"Rural practice was my idea," Dr. Burton said. "Giving something back and all that. But give and take seems to be mostly take."

There was sun out on the water, flickering in a loose semaphore, the air still, with the noise of chainsaws and car engines seeming to cut through the quiet from great distances. Ian looked at Anne, at the hollows around her eyes, and wondered how long they would stay in the town.

The phone rang four times during dinner, and in the quiet of the house, Ian listened to Anne murmuring softly, but sternly, into the phone, convincing patients they could wait until morning.

After dinner, they sat at the table without speaking.

Anne took their daughter away to get ready for bed, and Ian felt for a moment as if there was something that Dr. Burton wanted to tell him, as if there was an important fistful of words he wanted to bring up but couldn't force up his throat. Instead, the doctor told Ian a complicated story about how inshore fishermen had once used tarred twine ropes in their nets and often held the ropes with their teeth when they needed an extra hand, and how there had been regular mouth and lip cancers among fishermen. There wasn't a definitive link, the doctor said, but the cancers had almost completely disappeared with the arrival of nylon rope.

Ian was almost certain the story had more to do with Dr. Burton than it had to do with fishermen, but he was too tired to try and work out just what the point was.

After that, Ian said good night and drove to a bed and breakfast he'd stayed in a dozen times before and slept in the next morning until almost ten, safe in the knowledge that, unlike Dr. Burton, there was not a single phone being dialled that could possibly be looking for him.

The next morning he set out on the long drive back up the west coast of the province, watching each curving brook and patch of bog that shouldered in against the highway, and he wondered whether Burton and his wife were still talking about their quiet guest.

Ian had headed north, thinking about a limestone beach on the Northern Peninsula, a beach of solid pale sheets of grey-white limestone, and about the way individual plants—a beach pea here, a swamp iris there—would force their way up through cracks in the rock, barely any soil in sight, and throw their flowers up and open against the sky, a home in a completely inhospitable, hostile spot. Fighting their way through, imposing their own pattern of life. He thought about those plants all the way back to St. John's, a drive he had made so many times that he could walk through it on the backs of his eyelids with his eyes closed, although, this time, he found he couldn't remember a single piece of the trip by the next morning.

It was all chance and bad timing, Dr. Antle had said, sitting safely back behind his desk and looking at Ian over a piled wall of patient files with their multicoloured numbered tabs. The room looked like any one of a thousand other doctors' offices, Ian thought. Examining table along one side, a paper cover ready to rip off and change for the next patient, and the next. The disposable coverings made him think about disposable patients, even though Dr. Antle hadn't rushed him at all. It always amazed Ian how many doctors' offices he could gather up in his memory, and how often they had a low-rent, down-at-the-mouth feeling, like they were a business on their last legs. Except they never really were.

"Do the same thing a hundred times and nothing happens. Then do it just one more time and a cell changes..." Dr. Antle had a way of letting his sentences drop off at the end, Ian thought, like you were supposed to write your own logical endings to everything he said.

So it was all just chance. Ian couldn't stop thinking about that one little crucial starting cell, about how any number of things could have changed along the way. Maybe it could have rained on whatever sunny day it was and that little genetic squiggle might have turned left instead of right.

Maybe it was something more definite: some cell fighting the good fight, but pushed to the edge of its ability to fight off a looming blip of mutation. Then failing, falling over the edge, putting up the white flag, and surrendering. The cancer cells announcing, "There's a new sheriff in town..."

Ian thought about how there was a quick fix for everything. For his nascent cancer, maybe something as abrupt as a car accident, maybe some passing vehicle on a narrow highway cutting back in too soon on a dangerous yellow-line curve, the side of some stranger's car pancaking into his and slicing his hanging arm off. That would serve it right, he thought, thinking for a moment about how he would have to pull his belt tight around the stump with only one hand to stop the bleeding, and how useful it would be that his car had an automatic transmission and he'd still have one hand left to drive.

But Dr. Antle had also said "metastasized." He said it like there was a question mark at the end of the sentence, but Ian had registered the weight of it anyway. There was paperwork to do, specialist appointments to be made, biopsies and medical hand-offs to be done. Dr. Antle talked about fighting the cancer, but nothing about it seemed like a fight to Ian: just right now, it felt like an indeterminate fall down a suddenly steep hill. So he had listened, taken the referral documents, and headed back for the security of his car.

A dump truck passed Ian on the inside lane when he was going up Columbus Drive, and he realized he'd been hogging the passing lane when the dump truck driver carefully, and deliberately, gave him the finger. The driver was sitting up high enough that Ian couldn't really make out his face, just his hand in the window like a picture framed in a truck door.

There are a lot of new houses over there now, Ian thought, looking to his right. Rows of them. New houses, all put up at once, each one painted from a steady range of colours drawn from one single palette. He imagined what the paint colours might be called: Long Dune and Umber Sedge and Wicker Blue, all the houses built to fit together into some kind of synchronized whole. And there'd be more, he thought, spreading out in a slow-moving homogenous wave, a multicelled, developing organism.

Something had happened, Ian thought, and not just on his arm, either. Something had happened to time: it was already August, and yet it seemed that, only moments before, it had been May. Time was collapsing in on itself, speeding up every year faster, every season shorter. Maybe if I'd done things differently, Ian thought. Maybe if I'd gotten married, had some kids, but maybe that wouldn't have changed anything. I don't know, he thought. But maybe if I had a family, there would at least be someone to tell. Faces to crumple, because they cared.

Ian's mother had died first. At the end, she was not much more than a stick drawing of herself, wrapped up and lost in the coiling hospital blankets in a too-big bed in palliative care. Her husband—Ian's father—watched with what seemed like a permanently dazed expression on his face. It was like she dissolved furiously from within, her limbs in constant writhing motion, burning far more calories somewhere in her body than she could possibly take in by eating. Every day, she was a bit more manic: every day a little less of her there, until, when she died, she was just bones papered with loose skin. Her eyes hard like bright brass beads.

Ian's father burned up more literally: he died in a fire two weeks after Ian's mother died. The investigators told Ian the scorched cupboards pointed toward something—they had no idea what—forgotten on the back left burner of the stove overnight. But they didn't say "forgotten," Ian realized all at once. They said "left on the stove," a description that opened another door he wasn't keen to think about.

Ian, an only child, found himself caught up in the complications of two parents and their estate—along with the complications of what he felt, and what it was he felt that he was supposed to feel. Through it all—the legal work and the probate tangle left by neither parent having an official will—he stayed on the road, refusing to even take the eight days of bereavement leave, "four days for the death of a parent," times two, that his company's human relations policy spelled out. An HR officer named Susan seemed to feel it was her responsibility to bring him into the office and tell him that directly.

Susan didn't seem to understand his reply—that he wanted to keep on working, that he wanted to stay out on the road, that, despite all the things that had to be worked out, all the decisions that had to be made, all the paperwork that had to be filled out and signed and taken to the next place, he just wanted to get back to his usual routine.

Ian wanted work—just work—to stay the same, so that there was at least one thing, anything, that was exactly, precisely the same as it had been before. It anchored him to a world that, otherwise, he would have felt he had lost.

He drove his car down Columbus, his hands loose on the steering wheel, feeling the ridges on the underside of the wheel bump on his fingers as physics pulled the wheels back toward straight with no effort from him at all. Being in the flow of the traffic, he thought, was the way a platelet must feel inside an artery, speeding through to the next valve, pushed by the flow from the heart, no sliding backwards, out around the big circle, down through the small arteries and the capillaries and then back again, lungs and heart and everything else, touching every cell eventually, feeding, supplying oxygen, even to the damaged cells. Going, slowing, stopping even, and going again. Just like driving, the way there could be roadwork here, construction signs there, and everyone passing through the bottlenecks slowly and then speeding up again, everything controlled by outside, immutable rules.

At the last traffic light before the right turn for home, he caught a yellow and slowed to a stop. Ian watched the rear-view as the car behind almost hit him, coming up close enough that the headlights vanished from his mirror. Then the car let out a long, impatient blast of horn. The driver had obviously expected Ian to run the yellow light and had expected to dovetail tight in behind, darting through the intersection as well. Ian could make out only a few parts of the other driver's face in the mirror. Ian reached down and put the car in park, while his other hand unbuckled his seat belt.

He got out of the car and for a moment wondered what the intersection would look like from space or even from an airplane, a tableau fixed and flat under the pale late August sun with all its little pieces whirring and moving, so far away that every scrap of purpose would be too far away to be seen or understood. It would look like the seething world of pond water under a microscope, all sorts of life juddering in and out of the frame without any real reason at all.

Ian left the door of his car still hanging open so that it looked like a bird with a broken wing, the way he often passed a road-struck seagull or crow, looking dazed and trailing one wingtip along the surface of the asphalt.

He could hear the horns, and Ian thought that everything at the intersection looked cooked, baked down, the sunlight too harsh and battering down on him.

He walked back to the car that had pulled up behind him, a low-slung four-door, blue, its stereo pulsing fatly out through the open windows.

"What is your fucking problem?" the man in the car said to him. Ian felt detached as he looked in the window at the man in the driver's seat. The man had his legs spread wide apart, blue jeans, and a shirt open wide at the neck, as if he was absolutely comfortable there behind the wheel, as if people got out of their cars and walked back to confront him all the time. As if this was nothing in the least bit new or surprising.

Ian's sleeves had slid down to his wrists, so he slid them up past his elbows again, baring his brown skin before drawing his arm back and hitting the man full in the mouth with a suddenly formed fist.

And while it was happening, he thought of his arm, and of telling it: "See? That's what you're supposed to do. You do exactly what I tell you. When I tell you. And that's the only thing you do."

Ian felt the sun piercing his skin with every moment, like it was throwing out a million flaming pins, each one digging, seeking. His arms kept swinging, long after the horns stopped and drivers started climbing out of their cars.

ARMENIA

TOM GOT A BIZARRE and almost disturbing pleasure in sliding his hand along the rough and always-growing hair on her legs, but above the towel rack in the bathroom, there was a map of Armenia drawn on the wall in mould—small knots poking outwards above what would be the cities of Yerevan, Gyumri, and, down at the foot, Kapan—and Ray wouldn't let him wipe it away with something as simple as an old dishcloth and a good healthy dose of bleach.

She won't let him do anything about it, because she said it was a living thing. She told him that it was because she was a Buddhist, but he knew that was a lie, that her family was Methodist and she was, too, because she'd let it slip once in a lunchtime conversation. There were four of them at the table, and Tom sat silently listening, keeping the information to himself, not letting on that he knew.

The drain in the tub was so plugged he couldn't decide whether he was having a bath or a shower anymore, and what he really wanted was for her to be gone for an afternoon, just one single afternoon, so he could power a whole bottle of drain cleaner down there, then open the bathroom window wide and turn on the fan to waft away the smell, because no one should be forced to stand up to their ankles in soap scum every time they wash.

Then, if she asked him if he'd done anything to the tub, he could just shrug and say, "Something down there must have decided to go ahead and let go," and go back to reading, which was just about the only thing left to do in the house, because she had cut the cable off and the television only got one station and acres of grey-blue static on all the other channels.

Unplugging the drain would be fine, he thought. But if the map were to disappear, it wouldn't be that simple. Tom knew there would be no way to deny that he'd had something to do with that.

When they first met, she had said her name was Raisa, Raisa Grant, but she liked it when he shortened it to Ray. No one had ever called her Ray before, and she said she liked the way it sounded like she'd come from the sun. He didn't tell her it happened accidentally — that, all at once, it was like the last syllable of her name had simply fallen off his tongue. It was like his mouth had just seized up solid all at once and halfway through, unable to move.

Tom had met her at a film festival screening one night. She was taking ticket stubs and dropping the ripped halves into a small, overflowing wicker basket for the door prize, and he had asked her out right away, thinking there was no way that she'd ever say yes.

She had a raft of fine blond hair on her arms, the kind of slender, thin hair that seemed to move away uniformly, as if afraid, if you did as little as breathe on it. Cilia, bending and swaying like the heads of a field of wheat swept by wind. (Tom wasn't sure if there was ever going to be a right time or place to mention that. He was sure that there were things that you weren't supposed to notice, that, if you did, they would only end up being an unseemly fragmentation of the whole. High tits. Nice ass. Cilia.)

Their relationship wasn't complicated at first. There were no second thoughts, nothing held back. He had felt a kind of surge he wasn't used to, a confidence he couldn't claim as his own. She told her friends that they had just clicked, that they had shifted from acquaintances to a couple in a single night. He found he couldn't tell anyone about that without feeling a little embarrassed, as if it had all been too easy, too carefully un-thought. But she told the story more than often enough for both of them, told it easily in a this-was-always-meant-to-be way, as if the two of them were important enough that even destiny found the time and interest to get involved.

Tom felt differently, though; if asked, he might have said that they were like two cars colliding at an intersection and ending up inextricably knit together, a tangle of bumpers, engine parts, and steel. Two becoming one through brute force and physics.

But destiny or collision, they hit hard.

A mediocre meal at a vegetarian restaurant—cold spanakopita, the spinach reminding him of wet leaves just waiting for a rake—and a bottle of particularly resinous red wine led them back to her place. Her apartment was the upper floor of a downtown house that had been unceremoniously torn in two, renters top and bottom, with a shared front hall full of all the shoes and boots from everyone in the house.

Tom wasn't ready for the sheer physicality of Ray: he'd never been devoured before, but that was the only adjective he could come up with on the morning after their first date, the sun cutting in through the blinds in the clothing-strewn disaster that was her bedroom.

She'd been lying naked next to him on top of the covers, stretched out like a cat, the radiators pinging as the heat came on, the winter sun bright and staring, and he hadn't decided to move in as much as he'd simply stayed on.

She told Tom she'd had roommates, but they'd moved out a week before she'd met him. Raisa flatly refused to talk about them, except to say that it was good riddance. Later on, the timing of that departure would trouble him more than a little: what sort of "needed" had he been? But those thoughts came later. She didn't talk about her family, either. She told him she'd moved from Montreal and that things at home had been "more than difficult," but he'd mentioned that to some of her friends, and several of them had given a strange look, saying they'd always thought she'd grown up in Halifax.

His clothes and the few pieces of furniture from his apartment straggled in after him, a few at a time as they were needed, gradually settling into any open spaces at Ray's apartment. Tom hadn't intended to let his apartment go, but the lease came up for renewal two months after he met Raisa, and he realized all at once that the only things he still kept at his small one-bedroom were things he didn't use and didn't really need. His only stop there had become a weekly check-in to see that the pipes hadn't broken and a quick rifle through the mostly-junk-mail mailbox. It meant that giving the place up was less like making a decision and more like simply letting go of an old and under-maintained friendship.

No one ever said, "We should move in." It had been organic, natural, Ray insisted, like the mouldy map of Armenia.

Tom wasn't the one who noticed the Armenian shape of the spot. They had been having a party — red wine, lasagna, and weed — and Pavel, an Eastern European grad student, zipping up his fly coming out of the bathroom, had mentioned it: "Did you ever notice?"

Fascinated, Tom had taken a high school atlas into the bathroom the next day. It was Armenia, all right, only about the size of Tom's hand. Exactly Armenia, right down to a darker smear that corresponded with the massive Lake Sevan. He read more about Lake Sevan, about how it had changed after massive engineering attempts to both reduce and then rebuild its size and depth.

He learned the word "eutrophication" and read that it meant a massive growth and then death of plants, a rapid decay that starved the lake of oxygen. Stagnant water, so successful at growing that it actually killed its own surroundings.

For a while, he had an almost protective fondness for the mould spot himself, especially through the winter, when the central heating kept the air dry and the map dependent on the frequent mist from hot showers. Raisa liked long, hot showers, especially bent forward with Tom behind her.

But spring was wet. Very wet.

March ended with a heavy, endless slog of slushy snow and fog, and April and May were variations on the same theme. By the time June came, the front porch of the house smelled less like shoes and more like a heavy-skinned animal had crawled in under the bench and died, and now was progressively decaying. None of the shoes ever fully dried, and it was well past the point where anyone could blame it on another resident's foot problems.

The humidity was thicker upstairs: Raisa's apartment had no working kitchen vent, and Tom was pretty sure that some historical mistake in remodelling meant the downstairs tenants' kitchen vent actually ended in their kitchen somehow. Raisa could be cooking her garlic-laden spaghetti sauce, and still the kitchen would smell strongly of someone else's fugitive roast beef and gravy. She had insisted he at least try being vegetarian, too, but the smell of gravy was like torture, a constant reminder of what was now out of reach. The dryer vent leaked, and the space behind the dryer was draped with folds of grey, fibrous lint that had escaped past the lint filter and out the split side of the vent pipe, the moist vapour adding to the damp. All over the apartment, the windows fogged and then wept droplets of condensation, and the line of black mildew along the bottom of each pane of glass grew thicker with every day. But the bathroom was worse.

The smell of mould in the air was like a solid wall in the bathroom, and Tom was sure it must be getting a foothold back in behind the wallboard and finding a way onto all the surfaces in the bathroom itself. He was sure there must be spores falling like microscopic snow onto the wet towels every day after they hung them up to dry, like seeds falling onto fertilized ground.

It choked Tom up every single time he went in the bathroom: allergies he didn't know he had poured mucus down the back of his throat as soon as the smell of it hit. And he thought—he knew—that the mould was spreading.

In the bathroom, Armenia had arbitrarily moved outside its borders. On the left, it was invading what would be Turkey. It was, almost imperceptibly, heading toward Iran. Tom was sure Azerbaijan and Georgia would be next, if it hadn't happened already.

And still, Raisa had no interest in cleaning it up or having him clean it up. She did buy candles, fat candles with wicks that flickered at the centre of vast pools of molten wax, but the smell of the candles only lay over the top of the mildew. He didn't come out and say it to her, but he began to think her opposition to cleaning had nothing to do with the mould, and much more to do with keeping a tight grip on their relationship.

He hadn't noticed it when they first met, but she liked to be in charge. She had to be in charge. Sometimes, her need for control was subtle, but the longer they lived together, the less subtle it became. And it wasn't by sheer force of will: sometimes, it was more wheedling. A tone she had mastered that made him simply go along with whatever she wanted.

He stopped playing rec hockey on Saturdays, stopped the obligatory sports-bar restocking of the few calories he'd burned off on the ice. His hockey gear went down into storage in the shared basement. Now, Saturday nights were for book launches, film society movies with subtitles, and wherever else Raisa wanted to go. He was sure Ray's friends thought he was an idiot: he hadn't read any of the right books, hadn't seen any significant and important films. And when he talked about Raisa to any of her friends, he'd get quizzical, confused looks back.

Once, prying thick hummus from a plastic container with a failing cracker at a book launch in a dark bar, he'd talked to a bearded friend of Raisa's named Tony—a short, slight man who always wore a black and white kaffiyeh wrapped around his neck like a scarf—about the international work Raisa had done in her early twenties when she was volunteering with a children's aid agency.

"Raisa help kids? I've only ever seen Raisa help herself," Tony snorted before walking away.

Tom was beginning to think he'd never get the smell out of his nose.

He was in the apartment more than she was. He had a regular job doing clean-up for a construction company, seven to four, but she was working all that and more: a daytime job at a coffee shop, then some nights there as well, and often volunteer work. Maybe, he thought, she just wasn't there long enough to really notice the smell.

Once, when they were making love, he thought all at once that he had caught a hint of it on her skin, just on the inside of her elbow, where the skin was so soft that any sliding touch seemed to drag it into small, gently gilled chevrons—like sand swept into rills by waves—but the soft folds vanished as soon as he took his finger away. He pulled his head away from her quickly, but when he moved back in close and tried to smell it again, it was gone.

"What are you doing?" she said, going suddenly rigid.

"Nothing," he lied.

"It's like you think you're going to find some guy's cologne on me or something."

He didn't explain, didn't think he could explain. But a week later, he did smell something on her skin that wasn't mould. It was a sharp, almost salt-air smell, a deodorant that neither of them used. Then he remembered what she had said.

At night with the windows closed, Tom started dreaming about drowning, about someone holding the hair on the back of his head tight in their grasp, his face pushed down into a stream, so that there was nothing he could do but take great rasping deep breaths of water—water where there should really be air instead.

He would wake up all at once with his face streaked with snot, with the pillow wet, and he wasn't sure if maybe he wasn't crying as well. Sometimes Raisa would be there—often, she wasn't. But if she was, most times she was mumbling and restless, but still firmly asleep.

Unable to fall back asleep, Tom would lie in the bed, staring at the ceiling and imagining spending a whole weekend defeating the mould, at least enough of it so he could sleep through the night again. He was ready to strip the place down, wash all the walls, paint the window frames and any of the wall stains, but Raisa was having none of it: "It's my place and my rules," she said, seemingly unaware of the constant smell. "It's a living thing, Tom. *A living thing.*" He looked up dangerous moulds online and longed to tell her about the ones that damaged lungs permanently, the ones that required "special remediation." But he knew she'd ridicule him for worrying, and then all at once it was mid-June again, and the weather was suddenly warm enough for the old wooden windows to be pried open in their damp-warped frames.

June was also the month when he came home after work and found the apartment cleaned out. Well, half cleaned out. All of Raisa's things were gone, along with some of his things: CDs she'd liked, kitchen knives, all the rolled coins.

He called the coffee shop, but they only told him that she'd quit. When he went over, one of the baristas told him Raisa had told her co-workers that she had a job in Vernon, B.C., and that she and her boyfriend were moving.

"But I'm her boyfriend," Tom said.

"You're not the one who used to come and pick her up after work," the barista said, making a face that looked like she was trying hard to feel bad for him.

He called the landlord, asked if there was a lease, and if he could take over the apartment. The landlord told him Raisa's real name was actually Ruth, and that, whether Tom knew it or not, he'd been added to the lease three months before. By Ruth—or, at least, Ruth had picked up the papers and brought them back signed, "apparently by you. And, by the way, your rent is two months overdue. I'll need a cheque—this time, certified."

By then, Tom was sure he was pretty much ready for anything. As soon as he was back at home, he had the bleach in its big white bottle in his hand. Had the cloth and bucket.

Goodbye, Ray.

And hello there, Armenia.

BIDE AWHILE

THE CURTAIN LIFTED IN the window of the office—just for a moment. Something moved away from the glass and the curtain dropped back down.

The Bide Awhile campground had eight cabins. Small white cabins, two windows on the front, one window balanced squarely on either side of each front door. The cabins in two rows of four, the playground equipment in between.

It was six-thirty in the morning, the August sun angling in along the grass, catching small jewels of dew on the individual blades. Two crows were awake, calling back and forth from the roof of the office and the small shed that held the heating equipment for the pool.

The door of cabin number six was slightly ajar. It had been open all night. On the clothesline by the pool, a small pair of boy's green swimming trunks hung motionless, waiting for a breeze. Any time the wind shifted itself, the door in Cabin Six would rock quietly open and back toward closed.

In the play area between the cabins, the swings hung still on their chains. Two plastic slides, one yellow, one orange, were sheeted with interconnected water droplets, a skein of moisture, waiting for that one critical droplet to coalesce into a full-fledged drop and then ride down gravity's curve.

A small girl sat on one end of the teeter-totter, the other end empty and high up in the air. Occasionally, she straightened her legs, stood up, and then came back down to the ground again, lacking that crucial counterweight. Her name was Angie, and she was one of the four people staying in Cabin Six. Angie was five, and she was wearing her favourite sweater: white, with buttons up the front and a pattern of pink houses across the back.

The door in Cabin Six was not supposed to be open.

The door was supposed to have been closed and locked before Angie's parents, Mike and Beverly — Bev to her friends — Watton, went to bed. Both of the parents had agreed when they arrived that the lock on the door was too high and too complicated for Angie to unlock by herself.

Angie had wandered away once in a grocery store.

She was lost for all of fifteen minutes and had gained an instant reputation for disappearing. "Where's Angie?" "Make sure Angie hasn't wandered off." "Is Angie already in the car?" "Who's watching Angie?" "Sam— go get your little sister."

Making sure the cabin door was locked was Mike's job—part of their regular circle of nighttime tasks. Making sure all the doors were locked was always Mike's job. It was a familiar cycle—rain or shine, calm or storm: just like all the other household routines, Mike had the bathroom first   floss, brush teeth, mouthful of water, spit. Then Bev, with a more complicated, multi-step routine—makeup removal, floss, teeth, a final check to see that every feature, check to brow, was in place and in order. While she was in the bathroom, Mike checked the doors, turned off all but the last handful of lights, made his way to bed. Bev would do the last light—the bathroom—and make her way unsteadily through the dark, the familiar world bent awry by the click of the last switch. Mike was often asleep before Bev got to bed, lulled by the calm of regular and expected order.

THAT MORNING, ANGIE was still supposed to be asleep— that was also part of the regular order. But she had woken up, noticing the quiet in the cabin. Her brother,

Sam—the two of them happy to be sharing the same small vacation room—had slept through everything. He'd slept through the low, bitter back-and-forth of the argument at the small, plastic-covered kitchen table: Mike and Bev had been sitting next to each other, one corner of the small table between them. Mike had gotten up to get another beer, but when he came back, he had pulled out a different chair to sit directly across from his wife instead, as if making the combat more formal, the opposition more clear and diametric.

It hadn't been a quiet night in the cabin.

THE GUESTS IN Cabin Two, straight across from the Wattons, had heard the fight. So did Cabins Five and Seven. But they had all battened down the hatches as if trying to keep out a sudden unforecast storm, closing their windows even though the evening's heat still filled their small, stuffy, slightly mildewed rooms. They had all turned their backs to the rising voices.

Heather Weekes in Cabin Five did the most, asking her husband, Art, if they "should call down to the office." Later, she asked if maybe they should call the police.

In Cabin Seven, Anne Elton tried to force her children to sleep by reading bedtime stories far louder than usual, a strategy that proved counterproductive.

Oblivious, Barry Elton read the newspaper: "Story says housing prices are going to go up again," he called from the small living room. Anne frowned in one mid-, and over-loud, storybook sentence, but didn't even pause. The Elton children were under the covers, but wide-eyed. Neither child fell asleep for hours—and neither dared complain.

ANGIE GOT OFF the teeter-totter, letting the other end fall slowly toward the worn brown trench in the hard dirt. She paused at the edge of the sandbox, looking at the dew-softened edges of the previous day's constructions. A yellow plastic dump truck poked out of the top of a mound of sand like a half-finished sculpture. Plastic shovels sprawled flat like they had simply been dropped in mid-project at the end of the workday. The two crows had moved and now croaked back and forth from the tops of telephone poles on the side of the road in front of the cabin office: a third joined them, throwing its wings wide as it landed, feather-pointing to a stall in mid-flight and settling out of the air en pointe.

THE ARGUMENT HAD started, as many do, over money. It had progressed from there first to the easy touchstones that all marriages develop: those soft places where each spouse knows how to counter the other's defence, so it's easy to land a careless, glancing blow.

The argument had accelerated to the barren land that all couples know well but most steer away from: the blunt statements that depend on sharp backhands or even carefully chosen lies, the statements that are not meant for clearing the air but are deliberately meant for opening veins. For Mike and Bev, it started with a mutual loss of interest, anchored by the staples of who "was packing on the pounds" and whose "tits were on their way down to here."

There is a line. Every couple knows it, knows its feel, its shape, its shaggy, feral, dangerous smell. Every couple flirts with it sometimes in the heat of argument or battle, sometimes they get close to touching it. The smart ones pull back, swallowing the almost-said before it can burst out. Sometimes it's up to one person of the two to decide to harvest that one last small bud of caring, choosing to surrender instead, whatever the cost of lost and personal ground. Giving in, backing down.

But sometimes, neither can give up. And lines get crossed.

For Bev, it was one word, and not the harsh one of the two either.

Mike, standing up and heading for the fridge to get another beer, desperate and losing ground, threw the long—and painful—ball.

"Frigid bitch."

It was a single shot, made desperately without even looking back at her when he said it, and he only said it because he felt that he had few options. But as soon as he spoke, he knew it would hit insecurity's bull's eye. Unerringly. And it did.

The "bitch" she could live with. But the "frigid" was lethal, the kind of thing that cracked foundations, broke windows, blew shingles from the roof in handfuls.

It brought Bev flashing memories of him lurching away from on top of her, a dark shape outlined against the light-coloured ceiling, sweat dripping down onto her from his face while she lay numb and distant and wondering if she was the only woman in the world who had ever felt that way.

In one motion, Bev picked up the empty beer bottle Mike had left behind and threw it. She missed him with the first one, breaking the bottle into long brown shards against the cupboard door beside the fridge, but it didn't matter that it missed. The second one missed, too, as he went out the door. That bottle landed in the sandbox, unbroken.

They had a rule, one that had lasted for every single day of their entire marriage, eleven years, six months, and scattered uncounted days: settle every argument and make peace before going to bed and tumbling into sleep.

They broke that rule that night in Cabin Six.

Mike, already drunk, pushed out through the front door, slamming it behind him, the door crashing hard against the jamb and bouncing back before the latch had a chance to seat itself. Bev, crying and furious, heard the car start during her retreat to their back bedroom, but then forced herself to neither get up off the bed nor call out.

Mike fell asleep soon after, parked on the edge of a nearby dirt road, his breath slowly fogging the inside of the windows of the cooling car so that passing drivers—if there had been any—might have thought they'd stumbled on passionate teenagers too young to rent one of the nearby cabins.

Bev stayed awake waiting for more than two hours, her ears betraying her by perking up at every sound, however faint, but she eventually toppled into an uneasy sleep, dogged by dreams of running and falling, running and falling, terrified of something she couldn't escape but was never close enough to see clearly.

AT A QUARTER to seven, Angie walked slowly to the swimming pool gate. The sign said the gate was supposed to be kept closed: the sign said there was no lifeguard on duty and children under ten needed "parental supervision." Angie couldn't read. And the gate had been left open anyway.

There were drowned ants in the pool, scores of them, scattered on the light-blue pool cover that had been hauled over the surface the night before. Shallow water skimmed on top of the floating cover: deeper water underneath.

The ants were princesses all, cast out with their wings and their crowns and their former colonies' dreams, risen up from anthills all around the cabins on the day before, a singularly hot August day. Many found their way down to the regular light-blue chop of the surface of the swimming pool. And even their obvious royalty hadn't been enough to save them.

Angie stood on the edge of the pool, watching the struggling ants, while Bev slept in the back bedroom, breathing with a faint nasal snore, a gentle fleshy rattle, that Mike had once found endearing but that now annoyed him terribly. Mike slept in the car with the front seat all the way back, the keys still in the ignition, the headlights on until the car's battery was completely dead.

Angie knelt down, holding a long spear of timothy grass, coaxing a struggling ant onto the stem, bringing the ant over to the flat of the pool deck. On dry land, the princess was pinned to the concrete by her sodden wings, dragged down by finery and struggling helplessly.

Angie leaned out further over the pool cover to reach another ant. And another. Soon, there was a small struggling handful of ants on the pool deck—they weren't drowning, but they weren't escaping, either. The crows flew closer. Intelligent birds, they cocked their heads and waited: the fat ants were an annual tasty snack, and the crows had already spent time marching along the shoulders of the pool, plucking the closest ants up with their beaks, dead or alive, and eating them.

Angie tilted back and forth, rescuing ants. The crows waited. The knot of ants grew.

BEV WOKE UP and didn't hear the children: she hoped they were still sleeping and had slept through everything.

She looked at the closed bedroom door, and, without realizing, she imagined that it was still the same closed door, as if it had remained sealed throughout the night.

The kids had been tired, Bev reasoned, running all day at the beach, the pool, the playground. No, more than tired: they'd been worn out—they would have dropped off to sleep almost immediately and stayed there, sleeping the way small children do, as if drugged unconscious and then laid loose in haphazard, almost boneless arrangement. If they'd woken, she was sure they would have called or come out. The more she thought about it, the more she convinced herself they were still asleep behind the closed door.

She hoped they would still be sleeping when Mike came back.

FUCK HER. THAT'S what Mike thought when he woke up. He was stiff—his neck hurt. And he was still angry. I'll leave that bitch this time, he thought. Get a divorce. It would serve her right. Let her try to figure out the finances, let her put in the extra hours and then come home to the three-ring circus the way he did.

Single again, Mike thought, he would fuck waitresses until he was good and tired of fucking them. Tall ones, short ones, redheads, blondes. Threesomes. Foursomes. He'd find that temp, the temp who had drunkenly kissed him at the Christmas party three, no, four years before. He'd go online for dates, then tweet his exploits to a growing group of followers, one hundred and forty explicit characters at a time. He would go out every night—he'd try Ecstasy or speed. He'd be a party animal known for his stamina.

He would...go back to the cabin to Bev and apologize.

Of all the things he might do, that was the only one, he knew, that would actually happen. Even though it wouldn't work. Even though, he thought, he'd wear this one for months, all the more because he knew he'd have to be the one to give in. He sat up straight in the driver's seat, glad not to have been woken by the police instead of by the sun. He tried the key: the starting motor gave one tired sound and stopped completely.

He opened the car door, put one foot on the ground, and waited until he saw another car in the distance. Then he stood up.

He lifted both arms, waved at the oncoming car, muttering, "Give a guy a break, would you?" under his breath. The car slowed.

"Got any jumper cables?" he asked when the driver rolled down his window.

ANGIE WASN'T ON the pool deck anymore. The sleeve of her sweater was wet, so she took it off and left it next to the pool in the sun to dry. The gate swung closed behind her, and she walked back down through the cabins toward the road. When she stepped on the dirt path, her feet scuffed down through the damp of the dew to dry dirt: on the narrow concrete walkway, her feet left no marks at all.

SAM OPENED THE bedroom door and came out yawning.

Bev was sitting at the table. Replaying the fight again, her face blank, the corners of her mouth dragging the sides of her face down. She saw him, stood up, smiled, tugged at her shirt.

"Good morning, Sammy," she said. "Did you sleep well? Go get your sister up. I'm going to make pancakes."

Sam yawned again, confused. "She's not there," he said.

Bev jumped up, suddenly cold. "Where is she? When did she go?"

"I don't know," Sam said. "I was sleeping."

ANGIE WALKED BETWEEN Cabins Eight and Four, Seven and Three, past her own Cabin Six and its opposing Cabin Two. Past Five and One, and as she walked, all her attention was on the road. Angie knew she wasn't allowed on the road, but it didn't look that busy, and it was the only way to the beach.

You turn that way, she thought, looking to the right. You turn that way, and then you keep walking for a very long time, and then it's sand and waves and seagulls.

Just then, a car that looked just like hers turned onto the dirt road that ran behind the cabins. It swung by on the other side of the cabins just as she reached the last building, the only one without a companion across from it.

It was the office, where the lady with the keys lived, Angie thought. It was a small, stuffy place, and she'd stood at the counter with her father as he'd signed the register, listening to the heavy thump of the twin industrial dryers working over a big load of towels and sheets.

This morning, the lady wasn't there. The door swung open as she passed the office. The old man was there, the man with the whipper-snipper who cut the grass that shot up tall against the sides of the cabin walls, too close to mow. The man who would soon roll back the pool cover and expose the water's surface to another day's play.

Angie looked at the man: he stared back.

"Would you like some cereal?" the man said. He was holding a bowl: he tilted it toward her so Angie could see the last few cereal "Os" riding like life rings in a milky sea.

He closed the door after Angie came in, and the curtains rose briefly as if in surprise and then settled back into place.

MIKE WAS GOING in the front door of Cabin Six when Bev burst out.

"Angie's gone," Bev managed to say. They looked around, eyes sweeping the space between the cabins, saw the sweater crumpled on the pool deck, and started to run.

AT THE EDGE of the pool, the crows had arced in over the fence and settled near Angie's sweater, preparing for the pleasure of dining on the wing-pinioned, slowly drying princesses.

When the panic started, they took to the air again and watched from on high as the old man's car drove away.

BAGGAGE

THE STORE ON THE lower level of the mall had the cheapest suitcases out front—Alice knew that from experience.

Hard-shell luggage that looked like a cross between something a professional would carry and what a suitcase would look like if it was modelled on a wheeled turtle. Hard plastic, always at a good price—always the loss leaders, $100 or less. Alice had lifted up the ones that were on special, the ones that nudged out of the store and into the mall's open space with their signs shouting discounts. She'd checked their weight, felt their edges and seams, wondered whether the zippers would fail or if the stitching would unravel. She knew the more expensive ones were inside, the ones with the familiar brand names, with the Swiss

Army cross on the front, or the American Touristers with their familiar promise of secure and old-style travel. Leopard prints and pink ones and suitcases with bold stripes: as if you were supposed to show off some kind of surface personality to all those people who hadn't met you and never would. In other parts of the store, there were the purses and knapsacks and the computer bags that so many people seemed eager to shoulder.

Alice knew the way the aisles seemed to get narrower as you walked to the back of the store. It was as if there was a manual that dictated that the further the customer got into the store, the more and more crowded the place was supposed to be. The protruding cases and narrow lanes acted like sharp-toothed shoals, snagging you and keeping you from moving quickly when the sales staff angled toward you, alert, bright-eyed, and eager to make a sale.

"What are you looking for? Where are you going?" they'd say, pinning her deep in the store against the walls of cases without any obvious lane for escape.

Alice had no clear answers for them. She was without a decided destination, adrift. The sales staff were at a loss, too, unable to find a suitcase to fit anything as nebulous as Alice's absence of a clear plan. They would thrash around for a while before breaking it off with the usual, "Well, if you see anything you like..." It was, she thought, more an invitation to leave the store than it was to continue shopping.

Sometimes she would leave when that happened, just head right out of the mall and home to the Internet, opening airline sites, and booking flights that she cancelled just as soon as the screen demanding her credit card number came up.

Which of the eight flight options would be the best way to get to Vancouver? To Ottawa? To Brisbane, Australia? When she wasn't checking travel sites, Alice browsed through Las Vegas hotel offers, looked at B&Bs in small-town Newfoundland, and at a dude ranch operation in the foothills of Alberta. She tried to imagine having enough money in the bank or room on their credit card to pick a five-day or ten-day package, with only a one-way ticket. She wondered about news stories where women had disappeared but had turned up years later in South Florida, or Nevada, or the Northwest Territories.

But always, she came back to the luggage. It was a cheaper option, she thought: an easier dream.

What would be better? The big rectangular soft-sided ones or the small ones with the telescopic handles and the wheels that let them scoot along beside you almost like a pet? What would suit her clothing best? How much clothing should she take? How much could she take?

Her husband's name was Paul, and he spent the evenings sunk into his chair like a grounded ship. Alice tried to imagine what it would be like, telling him she was leaving. There would be two or maybe three new suitcases in a tightly regimented line next to her by the front door. She tried to picture the small living room filling up with the size of his angry voice. But would he even be angry, or just resigned, she wondered. She wasn't even sure of that. Would he start a fight or just shrug, his eyes barely flickering away from the television? When she imagined starting to explain that there just wasn't enough—enough contact, enough caring, enough *anything*—would he know what she was talking about, or would it simply flow over him like water?

Then she wondered how she'd feel after leaving—if she'd find herself missing the constant plodding regularity of their lives, something she was certain she'd grown to hate. She couldn't imagine that she would miss any of it. Not even Paul.

They'd met when they'd been teenagers in the Annapolis Valley, had married quickly in the midst of a pregnancy scare that later turned out to be a false alarm. Paul wanted to "do the right thing" and, at the same time, seemed almost proud of impending fatherhood. He didn't seem afraid—she was. He seemed, well, bigger.

They hadn't been going out together for long, but everyone said they looked good together. Alice remembered her friends saying they looked "made for each other." Somehow that was critically important to her at the time. More important than what they were going to do or whether their futures would come close to meshing.

When it turned out she wasn't pregnant after all, he'd announced that it didn't matter, because he'd wanted to get married anyway. They had already been to Canning to see the Justice of the Peace, a small intense man in a dirty office who had made Paul give him the $50 before the thirty-second instant marriage that left them with a certificate and, for Alice at least, a profound feeling that everything in the world had changed.

Alice was just beginning to look around the Justice of the Peace's small office with her newly married eyes when he shooed them out and into the small parking lot at the edge of the highway. She had hoped Paul would have joked around, picked her up and lifted her over the threshold of the car door and into the front seat of the Toyota, or swept her into his arms so they could hold each other in the warm spring air. Instead, he said, "Well, that's that, then" and walked around the front of the car, his car keys already out and jingling in his hand. But he did reach across right away and unlock her car door once he was in behind the wheel.

Alice wasn't sure she believed Paul would have married her without the pregnancy scare, and as hard as she tried not to let it bother her, the suspicion wormed at her. Alice knew him well enough by then to know that there was a way he held his mouth, a strange straightness at the corners of his lips that gave him away when he wasn't telling the truth. She hadn't told him about that look. She had always felt there were good reasons to hold onto an advantage, and it still worked.

At first, she'd thought that he was going to run his own business, because he was always so confident that his way was the right way. It would only be a few days into each new job before he'd come home from work and spell out the shortcomings and mistakes of his latest bosses.

This one wasted time and that one had favourites and no one ever stopped to tell you when you were doing a good job, only when you fucked up.

"They don't understand good management," he'd say. "They don't even know what it means" — and somehow she believed, at first, that he did.

That's not how it worked out: the bad managers just meant that Paul kept moving, job to job, always identifying the same flaws before moving on, never admitting that maybe he might be part of the problem. With each new job, she watched him shave away the sharp edges of his expectations — and hers — the only difference being that she felt like she was the only one who actually mourned the loss. And that wasn't the only loss. They had tried again for children and that hadn't worked out either. Alice, now forty, thought it was some kind of sign that they'd failed at the very thing that had brought them together in the first place.

IT WAS SURPRISING how many luggage stores there were in the bigger malls, she thought—surprising, too, that there were so few malls that didn't have at least one store dedicated just to suitcases. Didn't people ever have enough of the stuff? How often would you need new ones, anyway? It's not like it wears out, she thought. Not with only a trip or two a year, before being stuck back under the stairs in the basement until the next time you need it.

That was what Alice was thinking when a young man appeared next to her, "Robert" on a name tag pinned to his dark blue sweater.

He started with, "What are you looking for?"

She couldn't really blame him—it was, after all, a sensible question about a sensible kind of purchase—but it still made her sigh inwardly, as if she had hoped for more. But then Robert, a thin and awkward-looking younger man with a quick smile, surprised her.

"I get off at five. Want to go for a drink?"

She did want a drink and she didn't buy a suitcase. Not that day.

AFTERWARDS, WALKING BACK to her car after she'd met Robert, the thing Alice was most aware of was the wetness high on the inside of her thighs and the recurring thought that any single thing could have changed it all.

When they had gotten to the hotel room, one of the magnetic room keys didn't work. The other one did.

She knew with complete certainty that if both keys had failed, she would have left, walking out of the hotel without another thought.

There were a number of things just like that. The way one of his eye teeth sat slightly out of line from the rest of his teeth, giving him an almost hungry look. The way the front of his shirt—along the strip with the buttonholes—was frayed, slightly dark with wear. The back seat of his car, with a blanket thrown crookedly across the seat. Any one of them, or each one of them, charged with the power to change everything.

There were other things she'd noticed like small snapshots: the underside of the counter in the bathroom, the stain around the drain, the water glasses in their crinkled paper sleeves. The way the sheets felt against the skin of her back, against the backs of her moving legs. The curious way she felt about the whole thing, with him up above her, sweating and eager and separate. The dark room, with the silhouette of his hair ragged against the shadowed white of the ceiling.

Alice remembered feeling amazed that she was there — and feeling perfectly fine with being there — as he finished and crumpled down against her. She felt distant, not really in her body, and looked at everything as if it were new to her and strangely marvellous exactly because of that.

She liked all of that better than when he rolled on his side, turned on the light, and started asking questions. "I see you in the store a lot — are you planning a trip?" When she didn't answer, he said, "Do you live around here?" She felt awful for doing it, but she reached out a finger and put it against his lips.

"Shh," she said, feeling bad for a moment — but only a moment — as he toppled back onto his own side of the bed. She felt like a teacher in a classroom, deliberately and calculatingly shrugging off a too-precocious student and regaining some crucial distance. They lay there side by side in the silence.

Alice could hear his breathing, still slightly ragged, and she thought about the way the sharp ridges of his shoulder blades had felt under her hands. She wondered what was going through his head, but she didn't want to ask. He hadn't asked if she was married — she was still wearing her ring and hadn't thought for a moment about taking it off.

"I'll pay for the room," he said after another awkward minute of silence. She could hear something like gallantry poking through, his voice all high and thin and reedy.

"All right," she said, although she had never thought that it would be any different. It was easy and strangely familiar, giving up ground she had already surrendered. She could feel his sweat—their sweat— wicking off her body and into the air, leaving the skin of her stomach and breasts feeling sharply cooler. But she didn't reach for the sheet and pull it over herself. For a moment, she found herself thinking about spring sunshine and the way it feels the first time in the year when you realize it's actually come around again to warming your skin. She could also feel sleep approaching, stepping closer, but she got out of bed and got dressed before it arrived.

Robert lay on the bed without speaking, and he didn't say anything else to her before she closed the door.

ALICE HAD GROCERIES with her in the front seat of the car when she pulled into the driveway. The nice thick pork chops that Paul liked, green beans, a bag of new potatoes — his truck was in the driveway at the side of the house, and she knew he'd be watching television.

He was working different shifts now, taking plenty of hours at the call centre. A week earlier, he'd said that he liked it, that they left him pretty much alone. The only thing that really bothered him was reading the script where it said "This call may be monitored for quality assurance" and wondering every time if this was the call when there'd be a soft, hardly audible "click" and a manager would wordlessly join the call.

"We say that to the customers, but it's really supposed to be a message to us. 'Stay on the ball, we can pull your strings any time we like.' Like, 'We're always watching.' They don't know the first thing about motivating employees," he said.

That had been four days before, and it was, she thought, the longest conversation they'd had in a month, even though she'd said next to nothing.

She came through the door into the kitchen, put the groceries on the counter, looked across through into the living room where she could only see the edge of the couch and his protruding knees. There was a beer can upside-down in the sink, so at least he'd rinsed it.

"Hi, honey," she said.

She heard him murmur in response, heard him shift his weight. She looked into the living room — the knees were gone, but the coloured light from the television was still flickering across the wall.

"Good day?"

"Good enough," he said. "Shopping again?"

"Didn't find what I was looking for."

"Hmm."

She was certain Paul was already staring at the television again, that she could have said almost anything about her day and gotten the same response.

There was shouting from the living room, from the television. Now it was almost always reality shows, she thought. All of them about finding gold or catching crab or shooting alligators, or buying storage lockers and haunting auctions. Watching other people's exciting lives to make up for the one he wasn't living.

Alice took the frying pan out of the cupboard where it always was, took the pot for the beans from the drain rack, put the potatoes into the sink to wash.

As the water ran over her hands, she thought about driving to the really big mall that used to have the fountain in it, before they took the fountain out because teenagers kept pouring detergent into it. But when they filled in the fountain, they'd crammed in even more kiosks, so maybe, she thought, it wasn't anything to do with the detergent after all. She decided that was where she'd go next, even though it was an hour or so away, that or to the outlet stores that were all clustered at the highway exit coming into town. She was pretty sure there was a luggage place on the second level of the big mall.

When she closed her eyes, it was like she could almost feel a new suitcase handle in her hand.

OFFICIAL RULES
FOR POOL

TWO OF THE MEN were playing dominoes when he came through the door. As his eyes adjusted to the light, Matt Mahon realized that the sharp downward click of a domino put in its place had been the last sound he heard as the room fell still.

It was a canteen and pool hall in an old Quonset hut, the building like a great fat galvanized culvert split in two, laid on its side and set down awkwardly. Not only the building but the entire town looking as if it had been arbitrarily tossed out like a mat onto the great flat prairie.

Matt had never seen anyone playing dominoes before. Not formally, not seriously—not like the outcome of the game actually mattered—but for the two old men just inside the door, it obviously did. They studied the tiles, their eyes the only ones that hadn't

turned toward Matt and the sharp rap of the door closing behind him.

It was a strange patch of prairie, Matt thought. Probably the only prairie town for miles, maybe the only
prairie town anywhere that was surrounded by water,
even if that water was just an alkali lake, shallow and
strange-coloured and dotted with travelling flat-billed
pairs of snout-shovelling ducks.

Shelley was still out in the car, a rented silver Grand
Am with cruise control and the faint smell of spruce car
deodorizer, and Matt was glad she had stayed in the car.

There were six of them in all: the men playing dominoes; a table with three women, each with a bowl of
soup and a cane, and in behind, the two silent pool
tables sleeping under their bed-sheet shrouds; a woman
standing behind a hip-high Formica countertop with a
threaded pattern in dark greens, and chips busted out
all along the front edge.

Matt just wanted to use the bathroom, and maybe
get a cup of coffee.

He and Shelley had been driving since four in the
morning. They had a schedule to keep. Matt was on
his way to a job in Calgary that couldn't wait an extra
day. Shelley was along for the ride, like a girlfriend, he
thought, who won't let go of your hand, no matter how
awkward it felt.

They'd spent the morning filling up on beef jerky,

and chips, and other junk food, occasionally fiddling with the radio and stopping only for gas and to swap drivers.

The drive had started with a deep blue sky full of stars near Winnipeg. The road was straight in the way only open country will allow, and Matt had been at the wheel when the sun had suddenly appeared. He could picture the road back behind them for the whole drive, unspooling in his head like a dropped roll of ribbon. He occasionally nodded off in the passenger seat—Shelley driving, resolute, her jaw set on stern—and even then, with the steady whine of the tires on the pavement, most of his dreams had been about driving anyway.

There was some part of coming into Saskatchewan that he still wasn't sure about—like when the road had narrowed from four lanes to two and cracks had started to appear in the pavement, as if driving to a poor relation's house—but thinking back, he wasn't absolutely sure he hadn't dreamt part of it, manufacturing the roadway in his head.

"Chicken noodle," the woman behind the counter said. She was dressed in a white smock, grey wiry hair fighting out from under her hairnet.

"Excuse me?" Matt said.

"Chicken noodle. It's the soup of the day," she said. For some reason, Matt suddenly felt that the other people in the room were sharing a regular joke. There was only one pot, a huge aluminum barrel, on the front burner of the gas stove, the blue triangle flames flickering out tentatively from underneath the metal.

"Umm—the bathroom?" Matt asked, looking around.

"Down back in the corner," the woman said. "But you'll have to wait." She pointed back past the pool tables—in the gloom of the back corner of the room, there was a closed door, and next to it, an elderly man, standing, leaning against the wall with his palm flat on the wallpaper, as if depending on the straight line of the wall for his balance. The man didn't move, and Matt couldn't make out his eyes clearly enough in the darkness to see whether the man was looking at him or not.

If Shelley hadn't been sleeping when they pulled into the town, Matt would have made an attempt at a joke about its name—"Chaplin—must be a funny place"—but she hadn't stirred, not even when he shut the car off. He'd had an almost irresistible urge to wake her, to show her the cookie-cutter sameness of the town as they drove through it, the way the houses were all virtually identical, the way the streets had been laid out perfectly straight, as if planned in advance on an architect's drawing board somewhere a thousand miles away.

It was a company town, with even the small patches of yard designed with careful deliberation and the measured step of rulers. Matt had glanced over at Shelley, sleeping—her mouth went strangely slack, her face changed to someone both solemn and almost empty, like she'd drained out through a hole in herself—and he felt an odd little tug and decided not to wake her.

He wouldn't have even stopped in the town, except that his bladder was bursting, and by now the prairie was so clear and empty that he felt as if he would have to walk a mile or so from the highway just to get far enough out of sight to piss on the hummocked grass.

Chaplin had bumped up over the horizon all at once and just in time: one minute it had all been rolling prairie, brown and endless, and then Chaplin was simply there, a sleight-of-hand in the heat shimmer, appearing at the seam between sky and road.

It was an intersection and a gas station—but no one in sight at the twin pumps—and then the town out behind, a short rank of empty streets where the only cars in sight were parked in orderly lines, all on one side of the road. Matt imagined that, one morning, everyone would get a letter in their identical mailboxes, and the next morning, someone would carefully move all the cars to the other side of the street.

It was almost cartoon-bright outside by then, the sky huge and upended with only a few clouds running along the edge of the horizon. When Matt got out of the car, his hand had come up to shade his squinting eyes and he wished he had the ball cap he'd tossed into the back seat.

Standing and waiting for the bathroom, Matt imagined that the town was almost empty, kept up for appearances, and all of its residents were there in front of him.

Then the bathroom door opened, revealing the small wood-panelled bathroom, a single bright bare light bulb hanging above the toilet. For a moment, the bulb threw a thick wedge of light across the floor, and then an older woman moved out into the light, throwing a shadow across one of the pool tables. She had a cane in one hand, and as she came through the door, the man who had been waiting beside the door slid his arm easily through hers at the elbow, and they moved slowly back to an empty table.

The woman looked at him for a moment, pursing her lips slightly as if trying to remember how she knew him.

He let the two of them pass before he walked to the bathroom.

Matt was already out of the bathroom and up at the counter when Shelley came in. She saw him, waved sleepily, and swung her hip out to hit his with a solid little thunk as she walked by him to the bathroom, shutting the door hard behind her. He couldn't remember exactly when that particular intimacy had started — the couples' reach, the way one person always knows where the small of the other's back will be.

On the other side of the counter there was a long flat black griddle with a rectangular exhaust hood hunched over it. In the big two-handled aluminum pot, which was closer now, he could see big pieces of chicken cycling up through the soup's thermals, cresting at the yellow surface before sinking back down again.

There was an old automatic coffee maker: glass coffee pots with Bakelite handles and metal bottoms. Just looking at it, Matt knew it made hard black acidic coffee that he would feel in his gut for the next fifty miles. He bought a cup anyway.

"Sugar's over there," the woman at the counter said after he counted out enough change. Shelley was still in the washroom, so he put the plastic top on the cup and looked up, letting his eyes play slowly around the room.

The domino game had started again, the dominoes clicking like a dog's claws on linoleum. The players were two bushy-eyebrowed men, both leaning in over the table so that the crowns of their heads almost touched—the black dominoes sharply defined against the red and white checked plastic tablecloth. On the other side of the counter, behind Matt's back, he heard the tinny clatter of pot lids and silverware clashing.

Matt took a sip of the hot coffee and walked toward the back of the room, stopping to look at the faded cardboard signs by the rack of pool cues, two signs, each pinned in place with four thumbtacks, each with a small ribbon of rust running down the cardboard beneath them. "Official Rules for Pool," read one sign. "Care and Cleaning," said the other. Both signs had been made by the makers of the pool tables, and Matt could imagine the pool tables arriving at the train station decades before, flat and strangely heavy in their wooden crates, the big brittle sheets of slate packed carefully. He could imagine someone hanging the two pieces of card on the wall and then never having them move again, collecting dust.

There were chalkboards for each table, both with a shadow of some recent game ghosting up, carelessly erased handwriting that was still almost legible.

When Matt turned back, the coffee bitter on the back of his tongue, the woman who had left the bathroom earlier was looking straight at him, holding his eyes with her own. Her hands were flat on the surface of the table—faces can go two ways with age, Matt thought. They either fill out, rounding and losing their features in the depths of spare flesh, or else they dry to spare lines where every scrap of laughter ends up caught in the corners of the eyes, every angry moment caught in the thin space between the eyebrows. The woman looking at him was the second kind: her face was spare and lined, and Matt swore it was a road map of every right and wrong turn she'd ever taken. Brown eyes, now almost black, the whites around her pupils yellowed and strung with small blood vessels. She stared.

But with a little huff, like cool wind on his neck, he suddenly saw her as a much younger woman—hair black, those same eyes younger and flashing—the room changing, the pool tables pushed back closer to the wall.

Now surrounded by players, the occasional sharp click of the balls loud enough to break through the nimbus of cigarette smoke and music. He could see her with scarlet lipstick, a summer-weight dress falling just below her knees, broad mouth smiling. Outside in the prairie night, there would have been summer insects rising on the briny air from the alkali pond, the bugs battering futilely against the handful of street lights and the big dome lights at the gas station, the rising moon fat and yelling mutely at the edge of the horizon.

The picture changed; two people up against the back of the building, the man rushing, his hands low and eager, the woman with her back against the building and her dress pulled up. Two cigarette butts twisting red on the ground, turning like compass points with the wind, small threads of grass touching the butts, flaring bright into red filaments before winking out into grey ash. Then, their bodies lit bright for a few instants by the big light on the front of a train engine rumbling fast into town, shadows thrown against the back of the building and sliding down sidewise as the train passed. Her hands caught tight in the hair on the back of his head, everything fixed and sharp and frozen.

Then the train passed and the night was filling in again, simplifying the universe into touch and taste and stars and the slip of falling moon.

It ended, all at once, and Matt was sure he could still hear ragged breathing, and it might have been his own.

The woman at the table was still watching him intently when the bathroom door opened and Shelley came out.

"All set?" Shelley asked. It wasn't really a question—the length of her stride said simply, "Places to go," and he found himself immediately falling into step behind her, heading for the car, his path taking him right by the tables.

"Did you see it?" the old woman said, grabbing hold of the sleeve of his shirt as he passed close by her. "Did you see?" The man at the table was already reaching for his partner's hand, bending back each finger of her surprisingly strong grip one digit at a time.

"Let him go, Marie. Let him go," the man said, his voice calm and resigned, like this was an everyday occurrence.

Matt thought it might be her husband—the man looked toward Matt, his face serious but absolutely unreadable. "Go on," he said formally. "Don't mind her. Marie just gets all worked up when she sees someone

new. Upsets her when things are out of the ordinary."
Then he turned back toward the woman, the hair on
the back of his head silver smoothed tight to his head,
like wet fur on a mink or otter. An older version of the
man he'd just seen.

She was smiling now, but with tears bright on her face,
following the lines down. "I know," she said. "You see."

Matt moved away sharply and spilled some of the
coffee on the back of his hand, a small and startling
burn that grabbed his attention like a hand turning
his chin. Shelley was already out the door, the screen
banging back hard. Matt was hurrying then, his hand
already flicking the key to the car's ignition like a small
silver weapon.

One of the domino players snapped down a tile with
a sharp click, and Matt thought the sound could not
have been more final if it had been choreographed as
part of a disturbing and painfully short stage play.

Then the door slammed shut behind him as well,
and the bright sunshine hit his eyes like a wall, and the
inside of the pool hall simply disappeared as if it never
had been.

"Was there even one of them under seventy?" Shelley asked as they slowed at the stop sign to turn back
onto the highway. The turn signal ticked its ordered
heartbeat, one-two, one-two.

"I thought we were going to be trapped there. You

know, 'You have to stay here now. You are the future of our community. You have to stay and breed.'" She quavered the last two sentences in a high, thin, old voice, waving her hands up in front of her face, fingers shaking and pointing. She let her voice drop back into its normal range: "What the hell else would keep you in a place like that?"

Matt swung the car to the right.

"We should've taken pictures," Shelley said. "No one's going to believe it."

"You're right," he said, "no one would," and he was speeding the car up on the empty road, hearing the whirr of the tires and the thump of the wheels every time they drove over a crack in the grey pavement.

They were already driving past the very edge of town, the alkali salts high and white and piled in slope-sided cones. A yellow CAT loader was worrying the edge of one of the piles, its bucket drooling salt as it backed away, arms held high. It was the only thing moving at the salt plant, a rectangular building with high corrugated steel siding, the loader scrabbling like an insect building a small and traditional nest.

A train, three big Canadian Pacific diesel locomotives belching black smoke and pulling a long line of identical grain cars, was playing tag with them — catching them easily when the train tracks were in a straight line next to the road, losing ground again when the tracks veered away as the result of some small shift in the terrain.

The windows in the car were all the way down by then, and they passed a big flat-fronted tractor-trailer truck. It was big and too square and impassive, its windows mirrors, and Matt was reckless and swinging out too fast over the double line. As they pulled by, the trucker blew his horn at them. Matt flinched, but he didn't look back at the big semi in the rear-view.

Then Shelley was letting her long hair blow out the window, and she was laughing, really laughing as the yellow prairie whipped by. Matt had a last sip of coffee, grimaced, and poured it out the window, the slipstream catching it and flinging it against the side of the car in a long and trailing ribbon that would later catch a pattern of dust shaped like fossilized flame.

A hawk hung in the distance ahead of them, motionless — then Shelley was pointing at it, her entire upper body hanging outside the car now, the wind rippling her shirt tight against her breasts so that he could see the outline of them so clearly that it was as if he was holding them in his hands. The day so bright and full that it was like he couldn't stand it.

She was gripping onto the doorframe with just one hand now, her back bent by the wind as the car sped forward, pointing.

Then all at once the hawk plunged toward the

ground, angling down toward its prey, its wings swept back sharply as it dove. As it disappeared, Matt imagined some small life ending as quickly as someone flicking a light switch—a rabbit, maybe, or something smaller, a meadow vole or a mouse—a life ending with little more ceremony than an aerial shadow flicking down and a brief useless instant of alarm. An instant faster even than being caught in the cold, disinterested stare of a train's headlight.

"Did you see it?" Shelley called, the words coming in the window at him on a snatch of wind. "Did you see?"

And Matt felt a click in his chest, a small and solid heartsick definite thud, a feeling as if this moment would pass too quickly, and never, ever come again.

"I saw."

He heard the tires against the slightly roughened pavement as the car moved forward, the sound filling his ears, a noise so steady and even that it was as if it was never meant to stop. Matt forced himself to think about the future, about Shelley and Calgary and a job he'd taken because it was offered and because it was new.

He looked through the windshield and pretended there would never be a need, a time, to look in the mirror again.

SNOW

ART FORD HEARD THE snow blower in the distance as if the sound was coming through layers and layers of soft cloth. It didn't disturb him at first; he was warm under the weight of the covers, only just catching the sound of the engine rising as the wind blew it toward the house. It wasn't even annoying, but the more it cut into the edges of his sleep, the more a thought tugged at him that there was something he was supposed to be doing.

Then, all at once, he was awake, feet on the floor, all seventy-two years of waking and always being ready at a moment's notice, struggling to get to his feet without losing his balance, the window in front of him with only the curtains in the way. Before he even pulled the curtain aside, he knew what he was going to see. He knew it from the forecast, because they seldom got the really big storms wrong.

Fran was supposed to have woken him up—she was the one who was always up early, the light sleeper, the early riser. But it must have thrown her off, too, the sudden snowy quiet of it, the way the falling flakes seemed to eat the noise, swallowing it, erasing it.

They had watched the weather report before they had gone to bed, and Art had pointed at the approaching low pressure system on the weather map with one finger.

"Don't let me sleep in tomorrow," he'd told Fran. "Get me up as soon as you get up." Forty years they'd been married now, and she could always be depended on.

Now, he almost wanted to wake her and have words with her, but there wasn't time. Besides, looking across, seeing her sleeping, he didn't have the heart. She had never been a really sound sleeper, and he wouldn't think of waking her. He'd heard once that there is a point in life where you stop looking like a child when you're asleep, and start looking like you've died instead. Fran, he thought, had passed that point long before, lying there on her back with her mouth slightly open, her cheeks hanging loose. He couldn't even remember what she'd looked like before. Art would never have said a thing about it to her, though. He wondered for a moment what he must look like when he was sleeping, too, thinking that he was nothing to write home about either.

No time for all this, he thought, getting his pants and shirt from where he'd left them on the chair, bunching them all up and taking them to the bathroom so he could turn on the light and get dressed. He had no time to waste, not with the tax man already up and working.

It had to be the tax man, he thought. There were no other snow blowers on the street, and too much snow coming down for the sound to have been carrying from anywhere else.

The tax man—Art supposed he could tolerate the man, most of the time. They were both retired and shared many of the same slow, regular schedules. Except that the tax man was always trying to pull off some kind of one-upmanship. At least once a week he was talking about how lucky he was to be on his "partially indexed defined benefit pension" — or else he was doing something equally annoying like bringing Art a large double-double, without even asking, like Art and Fran were in such dire straits that they couldn't afford to buy a cup of coffee or something.

It was just as well that Fran was still sleeping, Art thought. He was already downstairs by then and pulling on his long winter boots. She'd only be talking about his blood sugar and trying to sit him down for breakfast or some foolishness. I can hear her now, he thought,

"Just wait—a piece of toast doesn't take that long. You can certainly sit down and have a piece of toast."

As if I could sit still even waiting for the toast to pop up, he thought, listening to the whine of the tax man's tired old blower somewhere down the street, hard at work.

Art had been out in the shed the night before, already able to feel the cold damp of the approaching storm in the night air. He wondered for a moment if he felt he could feel the incoming weather more clearly because he'd already seen it on the news, the young meteorologist cupping her hands around either side of the approaching front as if she could hold it up like clay and touch it, shape it. There was, he thought, almost a reverence in her voice.

He had changed the oil in the blower, of course. Well, more drained what was left and added plenty of new, because, while it was a workhorse, the blower smoked like crazy, a heavy blue cloud that Art secretly loved the smell of. He pulled and gapped the spark plug, scraping it clean, and checked to see that he had extra shear pins in case one broke. Then he opened the shed door and started the blower, marching it around the small workspace to be sure that the wheels were engaging. It was far too heavy for him to move without the powered tracks, and, he thought, it didn't matter how smoothly the thing was running if he couldn't get it out of the shed and into the snow.

He would like to have been able to take it out into the yard, just to push it face-first into a snowbank to see how the auger was working. The front of the blower had its share of dents and dings, and it would be nice to know if the blade was brushing the housing anywhere and whether the snow would travel loosely and evenly up through the chute and out. But there hadn't been enough snow for that; it had been cold enough, January already, but there hadn't been more than a few light snowfalls.

Art had watched bigger systems rumble toward them on the weather channel, watched them either waste away hundreds of miles before they got near St. John's or else warp and veer out to sea, either too far north or too far south to have any effect.

Before he left the shed, he took a rag and wiped the small amount of oil he'd spilled around the filler cap, and then rubbed away at the sooty dark triangle on the side where the exhaust blew back from the muffler. It was a mark he could never fully remove no matter how often he tried, a combination of stain and burnt paint from the muffler's heat.

He'd turned off the light with the blower sitting just inside the shed door, facing out. Ready to go, he thought, the moment Fran woke him up.

Before he'd gone to bed, Art had opened the curtains to see if there was any sign of the impending storm, but there was no snow falling then, just the orange of the street lights reflecting back from the heavy, low cloud. It certainly looked like snow, he thought.

He lay in bed and planned the whole campaign in his head. One straight cut from the shed down between the houses to the street, five short cuts for the rudimentary driveway where they didn't park anyway, and then two straight side-by-side runs across in front of the house until he got to the telephone pole that marked the property line between their house and Mary Tobin's.

Mary lived by herself: Art, dressed in his snowmobile suit and heavy mitts, dusted head to toe with powdered snow, would do the two long cuts in front of Mary's place, clearing the sidewalk, and he always touched his hand to his fur hat when Mary heard the blower, looked out the window, and waved her thanks.

Fran thought the whole thing was hilarious.

"She's twenty years younger than you are, Art. I think she could handle shovelling her own walk," Fran had said. But that wasn't really the point, Art had thought, although he didn't say it out loud. It had much more to do with the tax man, with his greasy smoothhandedness—and with Art himself.

"You're like a couple of old stags," Fran said, "trying to prove you've still got horns on your heads." The way she said it was almost kind, but it had the same feel, Art thought, as one of your parents reaching out and ruffling your hair, even after you were thirteen or fourteen, far too old for that to be easy, comfortable contact. He knew Fran didn't mind any of it, because sometimes when it snowed, he'd come downstairs and find she'd laid out his hat with the earflaps and his long mitts right by the back door, ready to go, the kind of casual mess that, usually, she couldn't stand.

The rules for the whole thing, he thought, were simple. You can't look like you're rushing, and you have to do all of your own walk, even the driveway, first. Neatly, too, no shortcuts. You weren't heading out to do Mary's walk: no, you were clearing your own walk—Mary's was just a courtesy afterwards, never the obvious goal. Neither he nor the tax man had ever put the rules into words, but they knew them just the same.

Other things about their approaches were different. Art blew his snow straight out into the street, even though the city said he wasn't allowed to. He always had and he always would. The way he figured it, if the city hadn't gotten around to sending a plow down their side street, then Art wasn't causing anyone any trouble.

The tax man had complained about that—in fact, Art was pretty sure that the tax man had actually called City Hall about it, because one year, a city supervisor's truck had nosed slowly down their street after the plows had gone by, and Art was sure the driver had been looking for any sign of misbehaviour.

The tax man was handicapped by the fact that he followed the city's rules — that he only blew the snow onto the snowbanks on the side of the street, meaning he had to stop moving to adjust the chute to keep the snow from falling on the road. The tax man also blew snow into the narrow front yards, sometimes so close to the fronts of the houses that they ended up skimmed with snow, like badly staged and tacky Christmas cards.

Art never did that, but he didn't tell the tax man why. It was because the blower sometimes picked up older snow with road salt already in it, the kind of thing that could kill front-yard gardens like Mary Tobin's. He knew that because Mary had told him.

The tax man had one other disadvantage, something that Art was counting on.

The tax man had an extra house. And a dilemma. The Fords lived directly next to Mary Tobin. The tax man, on the other side, was one house further down. Between the tax man and Mary Tobin was a big, set-back house that had had a succession of owners, each subsequent one paying a new higher price for the property and each sale driving up tax assessments all along the street each time. At the moment, it was owned by the Tofflers, a pair of SUV-owning professionals whose approach to snow seemed to be putting their SUV into reverse, piling backwards out into the street, and hoping that it would all be melted to a manageable level by the time they got home.

The tax man could make a quick double cut across the front of the Tofflers' house, or else he could loop out his own driveway, deliberately and obviously bypassing their place with a quick run down the street, and cut back in at Mary Tobin's.

The tax man had already soured things there by suggesting that maybe the Tofflers might want to chip in on gas some time, an offer they found baffling and a little insulting because they hadn't asked him to clear their sidewalk in the first place.

It was even more complicated for the tax man because the city had downgraded their street: it was no longer a snow priority because the city councillor who had lived on their street had lost the last election. The plows now came later and the tax man, even if he chose to take the street, would have to cut a path, even out on the roadway.

It was, Art thought as he went out the door, all about strategy. Tucked in there, too, was the element of surprise. The tax man, hunkered down behind his own noisy machine, wouldn't even know Art was out and working until Art turned the corner onto the street. The other side of the coin was that Art couldn't be sure just how much of a head start the tax man had actually gotten until he rounded the corner and saw him at work. Art knew that stomping down through the fresh snow to check, to sneak a look around the edge of the house instead of clearing the tight, clean path to the front, was cheating for sure.

Art opened the shed door, pulling it back hard against the weight of the drifted snow. He checked the gas, even though he already knew the blower was full, and pressed the electronic start. The blower started immediately. That's how it is when you take care of your equipment, Art thought, looking back at the single row of his own deep footprints from the back door. It was deep, all right: deep and powdery and still blowing around in a growing wind, the sharp edges of his boot prints near the house already softening and filling in.

He shifted the blower into gear and it gave a sudden, eager lurch forward, the tone of the engine changing as Art engaged the auger and snow began to fly.

He realized right away that the snow was deeper than he had expected it to be and that, during the night, the wind had swung around the side of the house, packing the snow into tight, waved drifts. The snow blower roared and the wind roared back, blowing snow into his face, the flakes catching and freezing in the bushy forests of his eyebrows.

It was hard work forcing the blower ahead, keeping the line straight, and Art was already sweating a little when he reached the corner, the blower passing the porch so that he could look down the street toward the tax man's house.

The tax man, Art realized, was closer than he had expected. It was going to be tight. But it was better when it was tight, he thought.

One winter, Art had managed to clear Mary Tobin's walk after every single storm. The tax man had been laid up after surgery, some incomprehensibly complicated thing that involved hauling great long ropes of hollow veins out of his leg and then putting them back somewhere else in his chest. That year, Art had even cleared the tax man's walk a couple of times. But it wasn't the same.

He was happy, the following winter, to hear the growl of the tax man's blower, to put down the cup of coffee he wouldn't have poured if he had known the tax man was healthy again and hurry for the door to take up the challenge.

The snow was still battering down and the tax man was chugging forward, his coat white with snow, blue smoke hanging around him for an instant before being snatched away by wind.

Art had barely finished his own driveway, while the tax man was already finished at his own house. In between gusts of drifting snow, Art could even see where the snowbank to the street had been cut cleanly. The tax man was heading along the sidewalk in front of

the Tofflers', the arc of snow from the discharge up high
into the bare black branches of the Tofflers' maple tree.
Art knew that the tax man had seen him by then and
knew he was in the lead, eager to press the advantage.

Fran must be up, Art thought, glancing at the now-
opened curtains in the bedroom upstairs. That meant
there would be eggs and sausage when he came back
in, right at the kitchen table as soon as he'd stripped
out of his overalls and jacket. He imagined closing
the door against the buffeting wind, the small gasp of
snowflakes that would blow in around him and vanish,
melting into droplets before they even had a chance to
flutter down to the floor.

I could just give up now, Art thought, but it was a
fleeting, almost treacherous idea. "Fords don't give up":
he'd said it, and his father had said it before him, but
Art was old enough to know that many things are in
the eye of the beholder, that it was possible to dress surrendering up as good judgment. He knew he could find
some sort of justification for almost any direction he
decided to take.

He pushed the snow blower into the snow in front of
him, taking advantage of things, he thought, that less
experienced men would not recognize. For instance,
there was a small natural dell behind the one telephone
pole in front of his house, a shadow from the prevailing winds that left a small, two-foot span virtually

snowless. Those same winds would also cut a rushing channel up between his house and Mary Tobin's. Sometimes, there would be a couple of feet of snow on other parts of the street, and the gap between the houses would be swept so clean he could see the points and angles of the gravel.

The tax man, meanwhile, was wrestling with deeper snow deposited by the swirl of wind from across the street. There was a spot there, Art knew, where you could even see the standing dervish of it, a little cyclone of spinning wind that captured snow and dropped it for no other reason than the unchanging geometry of the neighbouring houses.

Art knew it would take every single possible advantage to catch the tax man, who had the first cut across the Tofflers' property done and the second well started.

The tax man was still in the lead, although not by much, when his blower crossed onto Mary's sidewalk. Art saw the tax man's blower nose past the beginning of Mary's stone wall and he began pushing his own snow blower so hard that the tracks slipped forward on the slushy base snow, the whole weight of the machine moving ahead from the strength of Art's rapidly tiring arms and legs.

Art was seeing spots in front of his eyes that were surrounded, just at the edge of his vision, with a kind of darkening, like curtains left covering the edges of a window.

The snow blowers came together almost exactly at the foot of Mary Tobin's front staircase. Art could see that the tax man was also breathing hard, and thought about telling him that a guy with a bunch of straggly old leg-veins packed into his chest should be taking things a little easier. But he didn't say anything, mostly because his ears were roaring with the effort and because he didn't think he had enough breath left to get the words out.

There was still one cut left to do in front of Mary's house, but the snow blowers were sitting nose to nose in the first narrow path. Neither man reached down to shift his own machine into reverse. Blue smoke swirled around them and then was grabbed by the wind and flung away.

"I've got all day here," Art shouted over the noise of the two running snow blowers. There was sweat on his forehead: melted snow was running down the sides of his face.

"So do I," the tax man shouted back.

Over the wind, there was the sound of a snowplow in the distance, its blade harsh against the pavement, getting closer.

At the front of the snow blowers, only inches apart, the two opposing augers spun furiously, angry teeth in hungry mouths.

Neither giving an inch.

THE PATH OF MOST
RESISTANCE

DEAR SARA. (I don't know. Is that even right to call you that anymore? Let's say it is, at least as far as I'm concerned—Nell.)

I can feel the sun already warming the skin of my arms, even though it's only just reached the top of the hills, and the air still has that cool feeling left over from night. The sun is low enough right now—cutting parallel to the ground and through the constant scrim of pollution—that everything is far yellower than it should be, the reds and pinks of flowers muted in a way that they will not be after the sun gets higher and whiter.

The bees are out already, stumbling stupid in the air, and the roosters have mostly stopped crowing. The amplified public exercise class in the town centre has ended, the instructor's set of movements going only to eight—*ocho*—and back down to *uno*, so it's easy to imagine they must be beginners, a class where the instructor doesn't want to push them those last two steps to ten. I think of them on their mats, puffing and sweating even though it's February. We could have been there, stretched out beside each other on our own mats, the two girls against the world we used to be, a tag team, always ready to watch each other's backs. But now I'm here alone.

I'm in the middle of Mexico in the exact town we had picked, Tepoztlan, tucked in between ragged, lump-topped hills of volcanic pumice and hardened lava. The stone hills have been solid long enough for the trees to start to grow over them again. The hills stand out in only two dimensions against the flat matte sky. The tallest trees stretch along the very top spine of the hill in single file, like they are actually walking somewhere. Like they have some urgent place to go or at least some urgent need to see something new. So different, that line of walking trees, always headed somewhere else even though it's obvious that they can't do anything of the kind.

I haven't been here long enough to get my Spanish right. But I know enough of the language to know almost every time I've made a mistake, and not because of the behind-a-hand half-smile my mistakes create, but because I actually realize, just as the words leave my mouth, that I've messed up.

I know which churches ring which bells, although I'm not always sure why, and I know my way to the market and how much things cost and the rare occasions when a vendor at one of the stalls is trying to take advantage.

And Sara, I want you to know that it's everything we thought it would be, everything we dreamed it would be and more.

Right now, there are hummingbirds flitting back and forth amid a huge range of flowers— there are reds and purples and yellows and it's still only February. There are plants blooming that I only smell at night, with flowers so discreet that I can't even decide where the smells are coming from. The birds are all different, too—there's a sort of hummingbird sitting right over me now, making a racket but sitting still enough that I can see the sunlight coming right through the long curved needle of his beak. And there's some kind of fat, pink-bellied warbler that has been sitting in a leafless tree for ages, turning occasionally, and letting out a short little squawk every now and then like an important idea has just occurred to him.

The hummingbird keeps moving, but only to hover and start threading his beak into a flower that looks like a long red tube. If you were here, I know you'd be transfixed, that you'd just sit here, perfectly still, and watch him slipping his narrow beak into that thin tube until he finally finished and flitted away.

I mean, that's the kind of thing we talked about during all that planning, isn't it? Finding the flowers we'd never see except in photographs and spotting the birds that only live in guidebooks? It's everything we talked about doing. It's the world we were going to see.

When we'd sit on your bed in the apartment—and later our bed, after, well, you know, after—taking turns reading travel stories in the paper or in magazines. We were always trying to figure out the places with the best climate and the best prices, trying to figure out where we could go so that the money we'd saved would last the longest and where we'd have the most time to find work teaching English or lining up work with aid agencies. We spent more time on the where than on the how, because that part was more fun.

I remember when we looked at Africa and South America, one too far, the other too scary, and it was like Goldilocks and the three bears, both of us looking for the place that we could turn to each other and say, "This one's just right." Eastern Europe? The Middle East? Thailand? We considered and quickly dismissed them all for this small Mexican town, its name caught up with letters and sounds from a culture that only barely managed to survive the arrival of the invading Spanish.

Down in the valley, I can see smoke hanging over the tops of all the trees, white smoke that smells more like burning paper than anything else, but with a hint of resinous piney-ness, too. I know this particular haze is the start of everyone's breakfast, the charcoal braziers started for breakfast—"car-bon," stronger emphasis on the second syllable—brought to life with pine kindling coated with hard resin that glistens like a brown gem. We would have looked at it together and wondered, just for a moment, if someone's house had caught fire. I know you would have thought that— because that's what I used to think, too. But I've been here almost three months now, and I'm starting to know what's what.

I know I didn't leave any hints when I left. I didn't think I'd have to.

I flew into Mexico City and I made my way alone through customs and out of the city. That first lonely night in the hostel I remember thinking that there was no way that I would be able to even walk around here because it was just too frightening. The bus coming into town was packed, and through the window, I'd watched the heavily laden men and women trudging up the highway, and noticed the occasional water stops with AGUA all in white block letters on a water-blue background, as if the colour of the backing was every bit as important to its prospective users as the spelling was. Coming down into the town, all I could think was that it all looked so grim and dangerous, that no one even looked up, that they were carefully turning their faces away. There was no way I wanted to head out into it alone.

But when the sun came up in the morning, I had no choice but to go out on my own, because I needed to find something to eat.

It's eight a.m. now, and they just played the national anthem through the big aging loudspeakers downtown. They do the same thing every weekday morning. I didn't know it was the anthem, the first time I heard it. I was looking around, trying to figure out what the fuzzy, slightly martial serenade was that I was hearing and that stopped almost as quickly as it began.

You would have figured it out by now if you'd gotten here the same time I did.

You were supposed to be figuring it out.

I remember when it was all falling apart, watching you shake your head like this trip wasn't ever really in the cards, that all of our plans were never more than a game to you.

But it was always our plan, that was the deal, travelling together, "the two musketeers," you used to joke, and you even said we'd both be safer because of it.

So when I bought my ticket and you said, "It was a stupid daydream, Nell," I couldn't believe it.

Really?

It was no daydream for me.

I thought you were just afraid. That if I gave you a few days, you'd settle down and buy your ticket and we could laugh about it on the plane. Then you said that it wasn't that simple, and that you'd gotten involved with Josh, throwing that elephant into the room without any warning at all.

Even then, I thought it was just cold feet. Cold feet about the trip, cold feet about us, cold feet about explaining everything to our families. I thought that wouldn't last, that you'd come to your senses. We'd been planning this trip for three years, at least. Our last two years in college and then one whole year when we were working and putting away a nest egg to fall back on. Then, just when we were supposed to be heading south together for good, you bailed. You bailed on us.

I know you thought staying put was the sensible thing to do. I thought you were just taking the easy way out.

I regret some of the things I said that night.

I'm sorry that I said, "You start getting some cock and it turns your head right around, doesn't it?"

You know I don't usually talk that way. It sounded harsher than I'd meant it to. But I was angry, hurt, even if that doesn't excuse what I said. I was really angry — and I think I had a right to be. Six months earlier, if I'd said the same thing to you about some other guy, we would have gone to bed angry, and in the morning, we would have laughed about it.

And then you said, "A couple of times doesn't mean anything," putting it in the class of "just drunk and experimenting." I know we started slow and we'd only been sharing the room for a month or so, but was folding up my futon and using it as a TV-room couch most of the time just a better use of space and not really any kind of commitment? I shouldn't read anything into us sharing a bed?

My head was literally still spinning about that when, to drive the point home, you called Josh and he came right over and you guys went to the bedroom and closed the bedroom door like you planned it that way, just to make the point abundantly clear. There wasn't even a place left for me in my own apartment. I sat in the kitchen and I could hear you both talking, the back-and-forth murmuring low and indistinct through the thin door, and I heard you having sex before I finally left the apartment and started walking. I thought you were being deliberately cruel, and you were. It was my home, too, and you pushed me out. But maybe that was the only way you could see to break it off—maybe the best way to end any sentence is with a really obvious period.

Before I left, I gave away some of my stuff and I put the rest in my mom's basement for storage—I remember thinking, "Good luck looking for the big pot the next time you want to make spaghetti," and that made me smile a little. Just a little.

My mom was upset about all the room my things would take up, the mess of it all, the mattress and the box spring leaning up against the wall near the dryer, but I think that she wasn't really upset about that at all. I think she knew how upset I was, even if I was still putting one foot in front of the other.

I didn't think I would have to leave hints for you. I held out hope here for a long time. I thought you would be angry and scared and stubborn and then you'd realize that you'd made a mistake, think about what we had, and join me.

Find me.

It wouldn't be that hard. I'd be exactly where we were supposed to be.

I went right to where we put the red push-pin in the map, Sara, right exactly there, and stopped and waited.

Do you still even have the map on your wall? Do you have the same apartment? Is Josh opening your mail, especially any envelope with my name on it and a Mexican stamp?

I made it here, Sara. I got here and I'm doing just fine, with or without you. Just fine.

I don't know enough Spanish to teach English as a second language, but I've got enough to get hotel shifts at a small *residencia* that has occasional unilingual tourists and needs someone to answer questions and help them escape the regular, sometimes dangerous, shoals of mistranslation.

I have very little money, but I have a cheap place to stay and I'm learning Spanish faster than I ever could otherwise.

I figure six more months here and I'll be pretty much bilingual—and I figure, by then, I'll be ready to move on. The light will be familiar by then, the birds and their songs all expected and lost in the regular, the everyday, the routes to market as plain and average as your walk to the convenience store back home.

And Sara, if you still haven't turned up in six months, I think I'll move further south, and my terra will suddenly be incognito, at least as far as you're concerned. But I'm willing to give you that much time.

Even the buses don't scare me now, though I'm sure you'd be too terrified to even put a foot in one—the speed, the narrow roads—but I got used to it all, even though I know it's a dangerous ride every single time.

My plan is to go down the isthmus and maybe over into South America by June, just me and the small amount of stuff I can carry. Over into that continent we used to lie on the bed beside each other and shudder about, the names of the countries dark and strange-feeling on our tongues—Ecuador, Paraguay, Bolivia.

I realized, Sara, that I don't need you any more than, I guess, you need me.

But sometimes, when it's evening here, the last of the sunset has disappeared from the rock clifftops and the heat is evaporating out into the open night sky, and the dogs are barking and there's music—I mean, seriously, real *mariachi* music—and the sound is blowing up the hill to my apartment on the night breeze, I sit up in front of the open window, smelling the strange air, and think, "This is exactly what we were waiting for. This is what we wanted to have." Then something new catches my eye, and I can't help but want to nudge you with my elbow, just to make sure that you see it, too. Sara, you're like my ghost itch from my most recently amputated limb.

We were the constants, Sara, you and me and our three years of planning the future. The safety we knew in each other's arms.

I'd still be willing to try and find a way back.

Even if I can't figure out what the hell happened to you.

Love, Nell

THE REVOLUTION

THE NEWSROOM WAS DARK — the automatic lights worked the same regular hours that most of the reporters did, shutting off exactly thirty minutes after their shift ended and most of them left. Even the technology makes the point, Barry thought, the point that he was on the outside.

Barry could override the system, but he didn't. He liked the half-light of the place, only the fading sun coming in through the shadows, all of the computer screens dark, the pinpoints of the LEDs flickering brightly on the other machines that never slept.

Barry knew he'd been hired for exactly that shift: overnights, three evenings and always weekends. It had been in the job posting, one that almost no one applied for. Barry Keilly had been ready to pass up on it himself until the producers on the hiring board had suggested—without ever really saying it in so many words—that nights and weekends would be a good jumping-off point, a foot in the door for bigger things.

His foot was still caught firmly in that door. It had taken Barry a full year to realize that, desperate to fill the post, they probably would have told him almost anything. Filling nights-and-weekends was even harder than filling the posts in Labrador, and once they had a warm body in the job, they weren't likely to shoot themselves in the foot by letting him out of it. And then he'd failed at the negotiation, too. If he hadn't jumped at the possibility when they'd raised it, he might have been able to sweat an extra week of vacation or more money out of them before agreeing to do it.

But he'd signed on with the very first carrot—the vague possibility of some future offer.

So Barry came to work when the rest of the newsroom was packing up and heading for home or away for the weekend, full of chatter, and ignoring him almost completely in the hand-off. There would always be an email from the news desk about the things they knew were happening and the stories that would have to be updated, and a handful of scripts for him to read in the five-minute, top-of-the-hour newscasts. He knew that it hadn't always been that way, that once there'd been a technician in the booth as well, so at least there had been someone to have coffee with, but since full automation, everything was done in master control in Toronto. The only thing Barry had to do was walk into the booth, sit down in front of the microphone, watch the second hand tick to the top of the clock, and wait for the red light to turn green.

Barry would read five minutes' worth of news and a snippet of weather, and then head back upstairs to see if the police had sent any updates about car accidents or forest fires so that he could at least re-top a piece or two.

There was never enough time to actually leave the building and cover a story. That was for the weekday reporters, out doing full stories, the interesting work.

He'd never thought of himself as a journeyman, not even when he was doing early morning traffic. He certainly never thought he'd be on the other end of the graveyard, either.

Seven o'clock came and the cleaner rolled through while Barry read the newscast, "and in international news, military forces in Egypt fired on..." Afterwards, he went back upstairs to do a slow, strolling circumnavigation of the newsroom, once a pure blue ocean of industrial carpet squares, but now a sea that had developed darker pathways of wear.

They'd brought in the new desks with the carpet when they'd started using the newsroom as the backdrop for TV news as well. The modular layout was

more like a set than a real newsroom, reporters doub-
ling as extras in someone else's story. But Barry wasn't
ever part of the backdrop.

It was a slow night, as they often were. There was
a highway closure that would almost certainly be
updated before eight, but Barry wasn't in any rush. He
could have an update put together in five minutes at
the most. The highway would either be open, opening soon, or still closed, and there were only so many
ways to describe that. Everything else would just be
repeated, hour after hour. He'd check the main email
in case the police had sent in a release in the usual offi-
cialese — "officers apprehended the alleged suspect" —
but that was only a quick retype.

So instead of writing the updates, Barry wandered.

He counted up the desks of at least four dayside new
hires since he'd taken the weekend job. He'd applied for
every single one of those positions, had gone through
the courtesy interviews, the ones where the interviewers seem almost bored but duty-bound to interview
him because he was already in the bargaining unit.
He'd known the outcome even before they'd emailed
the "thank you very much for your interest, but..." He
could tell the way the interviews were going by the way
the interviewers broke off all eye contact with him, like
they felt bad about deceiving him.

He sat down at one of the desks, the one where a

perky television reporter named Melissa now sat. Barry knew she was waiting for her chance at a bigger job at national news. He knew her type: she was biding her time, keeping her stories tight and, thanks to regular exercise, he thought, her ass tighter. All mercenary, all the time.

He was so used to reporters coming and going that it was a wonder he could even hold onto any of their names. They were the movers, focused on that next crucial career step, every newsroom, every big story another important stepping stone. Proving grounds: a nice regional station to demonstrate how well rounded you were. There were pictures on her desk: parents, a couple with Melissa and female friends. One of her in a race bib, a marathon, of course; nothing less than a marathon or a triathlon was going to do, Barry thought.

She had no pictures of boyfriend or kids. Nothing to get in the way of being called out for the all-important forest fire or big-time downtown murder story. News stories with motorcycle gangs, especially Bandidos or Hells Angels, or better yet, a flood or a storm that would get her a little national exposure before the A-team got airdropped in. There was a script from her last story on her desk, but nothing else—not even a pen or a paper clip.

Barry reached down and tried the top desk drawer. It was locked. No problem, he thought. Seven and a half hours of shift, an hour for a meal break, a ruler and a letter opener, and there was nothing about the cheap locks he couldn't solve. The desks looked great on camera and hadn't been picked for security. The hardest part was leaving just enough of the tab up so he could catch it with the letter opener and pull it halfway locked again.

He'd be able to do it. He'd opened pretty much every desk in the newsroom already once or twice. He had gotten into the senior producer's desk so often he was worried that he might be permanently damaging the little tang on the top of the lock. But he didn't have to do that desk anymore: he'd managed to harvest the senior producer's email password (every time he changed it, the producer would write it in the same address book on the "P" page for "password") and it was much more interesting reading the producer's already-read email—and the whole "sent" file, too—than it was digging around in a fifty-year-old guy's pencils and old coffee stir-sticks.

Barry figured he was the only reporter in the newsroom who knew the station's entire budget, and the only person who knew that the last weather guy to leave hadn't really been dealing with carpal tunnel syndrome but with an entirely different problem about where he placed his hands. And not on the keyboard, either.

From his desk drawer explorations, Barry was the only one who knew that the senior producer ate his morning yogurt with the same spoon every day, before licking it off and throwing it back in the drawer until the next day without washing it, the bowl of the spoon constantly streaked with puréed fruit and dried yogurt.

Thank goodness for the open-concept newsroom, Barry thought. In the old days, the producer would have had an office and a locked door, and that would have been much more difficult.

Outside, it was beginning to get dark, the sun already down over the hill across from the station. Barry imagined everyone else in the newsroom at the same party, beer or wine in their hands, talking about the week that had gone by. "That was a killer week" and "I can't survive another one like that." Barry imagined being there, standing up, drinking and laughing like everyone else. Asking the new girl, National News Melissa, if she'd like to go out on a date, because they'd be almost equals away from the office, like soldiers in the same unit at the same rank, even if she was on the way up and he was at best treading water.

He imagined, just for a moment, that she'd actually said yes, and how they'd go to a restaurant and then back to her place, leaning back together on a modern and spotless designer couch, maybe even having sex in an everything-firm, everything-shaved TV kind of way: clean and gymnastic, seamless, sweatless coupling.

What I need, Barry thought, is a support group.

A bunch of the weekend and night staff from across the country, all getting together somewhere to grouse about how we're all being treated. What would we call ourselves? The Deadenders? Creatures of the Night?

But it could never happen, he thought. He knew they were out there, at least one at every single station in the country, but he didn't know any of their names.

Eight o'clock, nine, ten. A break until midnight, a sign-off to the international service at one, then home to the dead air that the night shift knew so well, Barry thought.

He got off work at the bendy part of the night, the time when he knew he should be sleeping but all his synapses were still firing, like live wires shooting off sparks. He knew it would be another three hours before he could go to bed without just lying there and staring at the ceiling.

When he got home, three hours of mindless television usually worked the best. A movie with subtitles, or something so mind-numbingly dull that every five minutes shut off a whole cubic inch of brain. But not quite the sheer pounding stupidity of infomercials ("And that's another chicken, perfectly, pull-apart cooked") but close.

Barry sometimes drove home so exhausted at the end of his shift that he would circle his own block, passing the driveway and forgetting to turn in—yet still unable to go to bed without spending some time disconnecting first.

They should pay us for that time, too, he thought, because it's a waiting game you lose if you get your timing wrong and wake up on the couch with the television still yammering and a stiff neck, the growing light of morning all over the floor like something bright had spilled.

Alcohol was always an option, but never a good one: cotton-mouthed, thick-headed mornings that didn't start until eleven-thirty were a bad idea, worse still if you'd gotten a couple of drinks in before getting amorous ideas and fondling awake a soundly sleeping spouse who would have to be up for work at seven. Then apologizing, and doing it again a week or so later. That kind of thing could only go on for so long.

And Barry knew all about that: he still had a fleshy ridge-and-dent on the finger where his wedding ring used to be, but at least after eighteen months the tan had finally evened out.

Helen kept the house.

He'd tried once or twice to meet someone new, but his hours just made it impossible. On the nights he was off work, his internal clock made him feel out of sync with the rest of the world: going out for a few drinks in the evening felt like an alcoholic's morning straightener.

Barry felt the need to connect with some other living human the way he imagined a determined salmon must feel, heading upstream. He'd even tried to make small talk with Melissa, breaking the ice with "I liked the report you did on the tent caterpillar infestation."

She had smiled back at him—that thousand-watt National News smile that's essential for a television reporter. If you're the interview subject, that smile almost makes up for the way they drop you like a dead fish as soon as the interview's over, he thought. A brilliant but empty smile, carefully crafted to promise nothing.

"Sorry, but I'm on deadline," she'd replied brightly. Even though he knew she wasn't. She turned back to her screen where she was reading the posted lineup for the national news as if she had a role to play in it. Barry wondered how she'd gotten access.

She's just waiting, he thought, just craving the chance to end a live report to the national desk with "Thanks, Peter" or "Thanks, Wendy." You don't even see the anchor you're thanking anyway, Barry knew. You just see the big staring glass eye of the camera lens looking back at you, then the cameraman leaning out and giving you a thumbs-up when the network has dropped the satellite link.

Barry spent the next day thinking about his place in it all. At least there was a live show on Saturday morning, another living breathing host in the building, but only until ten. After that, it was just Barry and the empty newsroom again. Barry sat down at the senior producer's desk, wondering what it would be like to have his job. He woke the computer up from its sleep and opened the email.

The first thing he saw, not unsurprisingly, was that Melissa was leaving. Not for a national news job, but for something closer to the nerve centre in Toronto, a lateral move except for the change of location. That was the other option, he thought: if you can't move up right away, keep moving, don't grow regional moss. Barry felt a pang of regret, then scrolled his way through the rest of the exchange, a back-and-forth between the producer and the regional director. Then he saw his name. The producer described Barry as "workmanlike" and said outright what he'd suspected anyway: that the hiring to replace Melissa should bypass even interviewing Barry, so they could keep him on nights where "we'll never find anyone else."

"Even the new j-school grads won't touch it," the email said. "It's career kryptonite."

Barry spent the rest of his Saturday shift going through the motions. The day stretched out in front of him like a race yet to be run, one where he knew he wasn't going to finish anywhere better than last. He didn't update any items. He just read them, looking at the microphone and trying to imagine people listening. He couldn't imagine a single one.

SUNDAY AFTERNOON AT one—that's when Barry decided the best time would be. He'd take matters into his own hands, he'd rebel, he'd strike a blow for himself and all the other Deadenders. It had come to him late Saturday night, his shift over, the daylight all fled, his living room lit by the television and a single table lamp, two heavy-poured Scotches in. He sat on the end of the couch where he always sat, and determined that, for once, he'd make the decisions, instead of being bounced along by the decisions of others.

On Sunday afternoon, precisely at one, he did exactly that.

Barry sat in the news studio and waited until the green light came on under the microphone, breathing softly, and then watched the second hand on the big clock sweep slowly through the minutes: one, two. The light stayed green: he didn't say a word. Barry didn't know what he expected. He wondered if the phone would ring later and someone would ask him why there was dead air instead of a newscast. Maybe they would just chalk it up to technical difficulties, he thought, the switch that didn't get flipped, the program or hard drive that shut down on an aging server somewhere. Three minutes, four, five.

Barry reached forward and turned the microphone off. It was quiet in the booth, the soundproofed walls eating up even the sound of his breathing. Barry gathered up his scripts, all on the thin green paper with the large type, and went back upstairs.

He had drawers to open, a spoon to steal, emails to read. He wondered what Melissa would think about the dead air. What she would say about his breathtaking lack of professionalism, about the deliberate implosion of what little career he had left. He wondered about just how foreign it would seem to her. He stopped and thought for a moment about his slightly-too-long hair, his scuffed shoes, the aging cable-knit sweater that was always either on his back or on his chair.

All of me must be foreign to her, he thought. Foreign and inexplicable. "I am the revolution, Melissa," he imagined saying to her.

But then no one called into the newsroom to complain about the missing newscast.

Just to make sure they got the point, he was silent through the two o'clock news; three o'clock and four as well.

Monday morning, he sat in his living room, anxious but ready, looking across at the telephone, waiting for the call that asked for an explanation or simply told him to come in and meet with Yogurt Spoon, the senior producer.

At four, he was still waiting. At four-fifteen, he felt the lead edge of all defiance running right out of him.

Barry packed his lunch bag and went to the front hall to get his shoes.

The revolution, he thought, is over.

COLLECTIONS

LEO SAW HER THROUGH the glass front door before she saw him, but only just, the light from outside backlighting her and marking her as a stranger before his hand was even on the doorknob. She was a small woman with a clipboard, and she was either someone to do with the election or someone collecting money again, he thought.

By then, Leo was close enough to the door that she would have been able to see him as well, even if he was only a dark shape behind the glass. Too far away to be recognized, he knew, but too close to pull back without being noticed.

He opened the door.

She showed him something that looked like an identification card, palming it so quickly that he barely saw the photograph, then tucked it face down under the clip on the clipboard.

"I'm with the Lung Association," she said.

"I'll get my wallet," Leo said, letting his eyes stray down over the clipboard quickly, trying to read if there were other donations from the neighbourhood, the entries upside down on the sheet. "How does $15 sound?"

"That's great," the woman said, staring at him and then past him down the long hallway as he turned to get his wallet off the kitchen counter. He was already wondering what was going through her head, what she was thinking about the open hallway and the dark arched cathedral of the staircase, wondering what kind of snap decisions she was making about the house, about him.

He'd been asleep when the doorbell rang, the television on and a blanket thrown over his feet, and he was still shaking cobwebs out of his head as he picked his wallet up—black smooth leather, a Christmas gift from Liz.

Liz was on the road again, somewhere in big-city Africa with only scattered Internet connections and occasional Skype calls that sounded like she was yelling at him through a long cardboard tube.

Leo was peering inside his wallet, walking back toward the woman at the door, counting the bills, thinking he'd have to make sure there was enough left for the groceries, when she spoke.

"You wouldn't believe the guy I ran into on Signal Hill Road," she said all at once. She also said it with a kind of finality, like she'd already decided that he wouldn't, in fact, be able to believe what she was going to say. Leo didn't even have a chance to answer.

"I mean, I'm a volunteer, donating my time, out in the cold and everything. And here he is, saying he'd give me $50, straight up, if I let him touch my cooch."

"What?" Leo said, his head still cloudy from sleep.

"My snatch. He said he'd give me fifty bucks if I let him touch my snatch. Said it right out there on the street, cars going by and everything. Dirty old man."

She was a small woman, barely up to his shoulder, grey strands scattered in the straight blond hair that hung down just past her ears, and when she smiled, he thought he caught a glimpse of one bad tooth, high on the right side of her upper jaw. The kind of tooth you'd only get a chance to see when she smiled. The rest of her face was thin, her chin pulled back too short as if her jaw was set too deep in the joint. Leo was trying to imagine anyone saying something like that to her, and trying to picture the sort of man who would have made that kind of offer.

"You wouldn't ever say that to anyone, would you?" she said.

Leo shook his head quickly. Behind the woman, the wind had rushed up the street, handfuls of grey-brown

leaves skipping crisply over themselves, their dry points
scraping along the pavement with a scratchy hiss that
made it seem like the street was suddenly crowded. It
was an ordinary Sunday afternoon, the houses opposite were quiet, everyone indoors.

"But then again, I'll bet you don't have to be paying a woman to get her to let you put your hand on
her snatch," she said, and Leo looked out through the
door, to see if there was anyone else nearby on the sidewalk, as if by some bizarre impossible chance Liz had
just pulled up and climbed out of the car and heard
the whole conversation. Liz wasn't expected back for
another week.

The woman waved her hand dismissively, as if nothing she'd just said even mattered.

"If he was younger like you, I suppose I would have
called the cops. And I would have let him have it right
between the eyes, because I can take care of myself. But
he was just an old drunk, so what are you going to do?
What's your name?" she said, her pen poised over the
clipboard, and suddenly Leo didn't want her to know.

But he told her anyway, he didn't see any way out
of it, and she took the address down from the number
over the door, brass tattletale numbers at least a couple
of inches high.

"They'll send you a receipt in a week or so—anything
over $10, and you'll get a tax receipt. Postal code?"

He gave her that, too, even though it felt a little bit like undressing, and she carefully wrote it down. She clipped the pen under the clasp with her ID, using the hand that had held the pen to push stray hairs back behind her ear.

"I wasn't going to tell anyone, right? What's the point? But then I went ahead and I told my uncle. He'd had a few drinks, and now him and Justin have gone up there looking for the guy," she said, her eyes fixed right on Leo's. He noticed that the woman didn't seem to have to blink.

"I'm Mary," she said, and put her hand out to shake his. Not knowing what else to do, Leo shook her hand, noticing that it was small and dry, but cold. In his peripheral vision, a burgundy van came into view and then accelerated past. Two more cars drove after it. It had been a noisy sort of fall day: the wind had been rattling in the newly bare trees, even a couple of half-hearted, sudden flurries of corn snow, more ice pellets than flakes, that the wind had carried in front of it like a thin sheet blowing along the road.

"How old are you? Forty-five, forty-six maybe?"

Leo felt there was no easy way to separate himself from the conversation.

"Forty-eight," he said. Forty-eight and married for twenty of them, he might have added, but he didn't. Forty-eight and well preserved in that three-times-a-week-at-the-gym kind of way that he almost felt was expected of him. Leo couldn't figure out why he was even thinking about it.

"My uncle—that's my uncle Peter, by the way—broke a guy's arm once in a bar fight. People think of it the way it is on television—bang, bang, guys swinging at each other's faces with big meaty fists, jaws stuck out—but it wasn't anything like that at all. His friend Justin said my uncle had him hold the guy's arm out over the bar, and then Pete swung a chair down from right over his head onto the guy's wrist. Not like anything's going to happen except broken bones. And cops."

She looked at him, shook her head. "Guy had a pin put right into the bone to hold it together afterwards, but I heard he lost all the strength in it anyway. My uncle and Justin and a few beers, that's a really bad combination every time."

Then she smiled, a bright, fixed smile that didn't hold any happiness at all, but that looked like she had practiced it carefully, dismissively. And that was, he thought, exactly what it was—a signoff, a goodbye, a thank-you-very-much, so other words weren't even necessary. But then she spoke again.

"Hey, you don't smoke, do you?"

Now she was holding the screen door open even though he'd already let go of it, one hand on the door and her other arm holding the clipboard in tight against her chest like a shield.

For an instant, Leo wasn't sure if it was a trick question, or what the right answer was — whether he should say yes and let her bum one, or whether he should say no, because she was collecting for the Lung Association after all, and she should be against smoking. He had the urge to tell her that he didn't smoke, and not only that, but that he was a runner, too, so he was probably in better shape than most people. Even though he still kept a pack of smokes in a kitchen cupboard, behind a row of cookbooks that never, ever left the shelf unless he needed to reach for the pack so he could go out on the deck for a quick, lung-filling release. He did it even though Liz always smelled the remains of the smoke as it hung around him, and always called him out on it, even though it was never more than one.

"No," Leo lied to the woman at the door. "No, I've never smoked."

"Good for you," she said cryptically, although there was something about her face that suggested she knew he was lying. A dissecting look — a look he knew well, a frank stare that un-layered skin and flesh, a look that reached right down to honest bone. She pulled her arm away from the screen door and let it slam closed. He watched as she walked away. She crossed the street, moving with a short, compact, contained stride. While he stared, she went past the front door of the house across the street, then passed the next one, too, and then she turned and waved, catching him flat-footed. He closed the inside door quickly, and she vanished behind the frosted glass.

At that moment, he was absolutely certain that what she had really wanted was for him to ask her inside out of the cold. That she had stopped at his house on purpose, by design. He had no idea how he knew that, but the bells were ringing in the back of his head, a clear thought that he should never, ever think of letting her inside, not even for a moment.

Later that afternoon, down in the basement, Leo was putting shelves up when he thought he heard the doorbell ring again. Liz had let him know that she expected the shelves to be up before she got back. She had a way of suggesting things that made it clear they weren't suggestions at all, more like directions cloaked in a softer sleeve merely for politeness' sake. He'd thought about the way she always invited him to make a choice, while ensuring that there was no real choice at all. He felt as if he were led by the nose, and helpless every single time.

He also knew that it was all a battle he had lost years before, lost so completely that even trying to fight it again was only delaying capitulation. Because he'd fought again, lost again, because she knew she'd win eventually, simply by holding her ground. He knew it, and worse, Liz knew it, too.

The doorbell rang again. He heard the one closing note. He was surrounded by sawdust at that point, fragrant sappy spruce sawdust that had been thrown out of the mitre saw and hung in the basement's fluorescent lights like static, granular smoke. If Liz had been home, he'd have been wearing a mask. Since she wasn't, he'd blow his nose later, looking into the Kleenex at the sawdust-darkened mucus with a small thrill of satisfaction.

He took the board away from underneath the saw and listened again until he was sure. It was the doorbell, thready and always sounding like it was short a critical part of its insides. When Leo finally made his way up from the basement, he saw that it was the Lung Association woman again. Mary.

She held her clipboard out in front of her, like she needed a barrier between them.

"I forgot what to put on the receipt. It was $50, right? They'll send it in a week or so."

"It was $15, sure." Leo could feel himself smiling at the mistake, could feel his lips pulling up at the corners as if they had nothing to do with him.

"Was it now? You're sure?"

And she looked sharply at him, measuring. She only paused for an instant.

"You know, my uncle still hasn't found that guy. They've been all up and down the hill, and they haven't been able to find where he lives. And they've got a pretty good head of steam on, too."

"What's that got to do with me?" Leo said.

"I don't know. I just know they're looking, and when they're looking, they like to find something. And sooner or later they'll be asking me, 'You sure it was Signal Hill Road?' Maybe they'll be asking if it was this street. Like if I was confused, and it was one of your neighbours or something. I mean, I've been a lot of places, one house looks like the next—I could've gotten it wrong."

"So what is this about?" Leo said sharply. "Some kind of shakedown?" He was trying to sound angry, but he was suddenly tired. He knew he had to be firm, but felt the resolve fast running out of him like water down an open drain.

She smiled again, a real smile this time, and he caught another glimpse of that tooth, dark enough that it looked almost grey at the root. He was watching her face, and saw the way her eyes hardened into an appraising stare before her face cleared again.

"No. But are you good at lying?" she said bluntly. "Are you going to be able to convince my drunk uncle that it's the first time you've heard about any of this? You don't even have to try to answer that."

Leo reached for his wallet, hoping that there actually would be $35 left in there.

She laughed at him when she took the money.

"And poor you. You didn't even get to have your feel," she said. She cycled her hips crudely toward him just once, her mouth hanging open as if she was panting, before letting the screen door slam back hard on his arm, the arm he'd somehow forgotten to put back down by his side.

"See you," she called back to him without even looking.

Leo remained at the door long after she'd left. The day had changed, he thought. It had, sometime in the afternoon, crossed the line between fall and winter — from now on, the snow wouldn't be tentative sweeps across the pavement. It's exactly like that line, he thought, between when someone barely knows you, and the point when you know each other all too well. The other side of the line when you stop telling each other stories about your earlier lives, and start any conversation with the shorthand you both know, and don't even enjoy anymore. Where you don't even have to talk to each other to know exactly what's going to happen, what direction everything's going in, where everything's going to end.

He finished the shelves that weekend, and the following Saturday morning was starting on the varnish. Three coats, just enough time left for the last one to be dry and the basement all aired out before her flight came in, and he would, of course, meet Liz, her luggage and her intercontinental exhaustion, at the airport, right on time, just like he was supposed to.

The first coat was done, tacky to the touch, when the doorbell rang.

"Collecting for the Heart and Stroke now," Mary said.

Leo saw the top of a fresh DuMaurier cigarette package lipping out of her jacket pocket like a rude red tongue, and he knew that it was there to call him a liar. She'd given up even the pretence of carrying the clipboard.

"I'm thinking another $50."

DARDEN PLACE

"THERE THEY GO AGAIN. It's so cute!" Anne Warner said, her voice thrown high at "cute."

She was holding a cup of coffee and looking out through the front window into the cul-de-sac, watching Mrs. Anderson and Roxy slowly make their way up Darden Place, the leash between them limp in a long downward loop and dragging along the road. Mrs. Anderson was wearing her springtime beige duffle coat, Roxy a tattered burgundy dog jacket.

"They look so much alike — they even have the same haircut," Anne said to her husband, Mike, who was back behind her in the kitchen. And they did, Roxy with her downward terrier face, the hair on her small head falling away to the sides of her ears, and Mrs. Anderson with her grey hair cut in an easy-to-care-for short wedge.

The pair was moving slowly, and from behind, they had the same stiff-hipped back-and-forth slow rock.

"Rain or shine, they won't miss their walk," Anne said.

In the kitchen, Mike grunted, struggling with the coffee machine. "Isn't it supposed to stop dripping when you take the pot out?" he said, irritation clear in his voice. "Damn useless imported useless crap."

HELEN ANDERSON HAD cinched the dog jacket on, clipped the leash onto Roxy's collar before she opened the door, not that there was any danger that Roxy was going to dart outside into traffic: there wasn't any traffic at the end of the cul-de-sac, and Roxy was too old and slow to be darting anywhere. The vet had told Mrs. Anderson that Roxy's hip was arthritic. The doctor hadn't said anything about Mrs. Anderson's hip, because she hadn't asked. The extendable leash always hung on the hook closest to the door to the driveway, right next to Helen's husband David's coat. David's coat wasn't going anywhere, either, Helen thought—David was gone, dead for six months now, but his things were still all over the house, essentially where they had fallen or, more often, where they still fit.

"Time for a walk, Roxy?" she said. Roxy looked at her with round wet brown eyes—intelligent but unable to express anything more about what the dog was thinking—and whined softly. Roxy's pink tongue licked out around her mouth, where the hair was a dirty brown like she'd been eating messily, and then tucked back in.

Out on her driveway, Helen stopped for a moment, looking at the street. Roxy kept ambling forward, pulling the retractable leash out slowly as she walked. Eight houses both sides, Helen thought, and we used to be friends with all of them. Used to know all of their stories, too: Alan Weeks with the rude mouth when he'd had too many drinks, married to long-suffering Ellen; Barb and Mark the competitive gardeners; Wally and Juliet Allwood—Juliet, Helen thought, making up for her virginal Shakespearean name by dressing like the neighbourhood slut well into her late fifties.

All summer long, it was one barbecue after another, everyone taking turns to be the ones to buy the wine and make the dinner, the others on rotation bringing bread, salad, dessert. David used to call it "the camino de San Darden."

"The shortest and most sacrilegious pilgrimage in the world, with the added benefit that you never need a taxi home," he'd say, smiling as if the same old line could never get tired.

At least the grass is green now, Helen thought, even if it's still cold out. She started forward, pressed the button on the leash handle, the spring winding in some of the slack. Roxy's even, plodding pace didn't change. There was a time when Roxy used to strain against the leash, urgently trying to find the sources of the things she was smelling. Then again, Helen thought, there was a time when we were all straining against the leash.

They took the same stumping walk every day: up to the top of Darden walking on the street, then left onto the sidewalk at Prine. They were so used to it that Roxy almost always stopped to pee in the same two places, and Helen didn't have to get the plastic bag out until they were almost home again.

Roxy didn't change her pace, always followed the same pattern: she'd pee, take a step forward, then her back legs would reflexively flick back and forth—one, two, three, four times—as if burying any trace of her own urine, but only managing to decorate it with blades of torn grass.

They came around the corner as the letter carrier came the other way—the mailman was a mailwoman now, Helen thought—and the woman bent down and let Roxy smell her hand before ruffling the dog's ears and scratching the white dog under her chin.

"She's gorgeous," the letter carrier said. "What's her name?"

"Roxy—she's a Westie, a West Highland terrier. They're a very smart breed."

"You can tell."

Roxy looked back and forth at the two women, then started forward, unravelling the leash.

"She always makes a dignified exit," Helen said.

There was an awkward pause.

"That's a skill most of us are missing," the letter carrier said. She waved as she walked away, and then ordered the letters in her hand as she turned onto Darden.

One by one, the guard has changed at every single house but ours, Helen thought, wondering, as she had before, if there was some crucial point of timing she and David had missed.

Juliet and Wally first: they had cashed out when real estate prices were high and Wally had a prostate cancer scare — "I'm not shovelling that driveway by myself all winter," Juliet had told Helen, saying they had their eye on a seniors' condo. "We're just ready," Juliet had said, while Helen looked at the deep open vee of Juliet's blouse and wondered how ready the other condominium owners were going to be for her.

At first Helen and David thought their new neighbours were less concerned about the perfect party and more about the perfect lawn; for the first few months, the new owners appeared only to pry weeds from the grass with a variety of medieval-looking tools, long-handled and short-, the digging almost ritualistic. Their

names were Beth and Tony, and they barely had time
to say hello.

One night, Helen and David had gotten a little
tipsy and David had said they should go out and collect
bunches of the white-parachuted seeds from the dan-
delions in their backyard. "We could go across under
cover of darkness and start shaking seeds on their lawn,
just so that they'll still have something to do next year."
He laughed until the coughing started. He could cough
until his lips changed colour, looking like they were
stained with juice from blackberries.

He was calling his lungs "the pipes" by then, and
would talk about how, when it was damp, it was a bad
day for the pipes, and the first spring after his diagnosis,
it was always damp. Helen would wake up and hear
him coughing raggedly in the front bedroom — he'd
creep so quietly out of bed that she wouldn't feel the
mattress move, and would only startle awake if he
didn't manage to stifle the upwelling cough for long
enough to get almost out of earshot.

"Pipes aren't happy," he'd say when she asked how
he was feeling.

David's doctor had been blunt: "It's not the kind of
thing that gets better. Your best option—your very
best option—is for it not to get worse quickly. But it
will get worse."

It did—not so much at first, and in fits and starts,

but it wasn't long before David was on oxygen whether he was awake or asleep, a plastic umbilical cord connecting him to the tank.

The next couple to go were the gardeners: Barb and Mark sold their now-too-big house with the ornamental crabapple trees on either side of the driveway to two lawyers, a professional couple who promptly cut down one of the trees so that they could widen the driveway and park side by side and never have to move each other's car. Helen thought the missing crabapple tree made the house look strangely unbalanced: she also thought the garden under the front window, especially the irises, could use a weeding, at least until the lawyers hired a company to come in and pull everything out and replace it with no-fuss creeping ground cover.

At first, they tried: the new families and the older couples had a few parties where everybody was invited, but it was like a junior high dance where the boys lined up along one side of the gym and the girls on the other, no one willing to be the first to cross the wide-open space between.

The new people seemed to have much more in common with each other: the older residents stayed in a knot at one end of the living room while at the other, the couples all talked too loudly about how smart their children were.

Then overbearing Alan Weeks died and Ellen came
out of her shell all at once. She'd had too much to drink
and then lost it altogether over a quinoa Greek salad
at the last all-street party they were all invited to: "For
Christ's sake, what's next? If the Peruvians ate bird
shit, would we have to spend months eating that, too?"
Then she tried to come on to both the lawyers — male
and female, and twenty years younger than her — and
threw up spectacularly on the hood of someone's car,
and, after the vodka ran out, teetered sideways, crying,
down the driveway toward number 6.

After that, David and Helen heard parties on the
street from the couch in their living room, watching out
the big 1970s picture window as the tide of new neighbours, more and more it seemed every time, washed
home like sea wrack heading for the tide line. Even at
that point, David could still handle the short walk up
and down the street, the wheeled tank behind him like
his own small dog, but he knew people found it unset-
tling, the occasional hiss, the rough hospital-like join
of nose to plastic tubing. The in-your-face mortality of
it all.

"We didn't insult anyone's salad," Helen complained
one evening, looking through the gap in the curtains
at the newest couple walking by with a saran-covered
glass salad bowl. "No," David said, the air hissing softly
in the silent room. "We insulted them by association."

Still, Helen had laughed a couple of weeks later when they were sitting on the back deck in the sun and David deadpanned, "Look—a robin's gone and done his quinoa on the railing."

Doing anything away from the street was even harder—wrestling the tank in and out of the car, making sure there was enough oxygen, the worry about whether there would be parking within David's limited walking distance—so they hardly went anywhere at all. Helen handled the shopping and got the car serviced. David paid the bills and circled the house at the end of his plastic tether. Helen was almost sure she could see the line at the very edge of the hose's reach, like grass pounded down by a chained dog.

The sicker David got, the less she saw people on the street. They would wave, but it was almost as if they would speed up if they saw her coming around the corner with Roxy, hurrying indoors to avoid contagion. And then number 1 went up for sale, the Brysons', and even though Art and Eve Bryson had always been on the edge of the neighbourhood social circle, it seemed like the end of an entire era to Helen. At that point, David wasn't going anywhere anyway, but the sale of number 1 still seemed as final as a slammed door.

David's death, as it turned out, just felt like a piece of the changing neighbourhood; Helen hadn't been waiting for it, but she had been expecting it, in the same way that when a clock keeps losing more and more time, you're not surprised to wake up one morning and find that it has completely stopped.

She woke up and found David, but Helen kept that to herself: she didn't think there was another person in the world who could share the complete horror of it.

Juliet came by afterwards with a lasagna and a very short black skirt. Barb and Mark sent a condolence card from rural Nova Scotia, where they had bought a two-hundred-year-old farmhouse that seemed to specialize in falling down around their ears.

The new people on the street stopped and offered their condolences when Helen and Roxy ran into them while walking.

ANNE WATCHED HELEN coming back down the street and turned toward the kitchen again, to where Mike was back fussing with the coffee maker.

"Next time I bake, I should take her some fresh cookies," she said. "I can't imagine she's doing any baking for herself these days."

Roxy ambled into the end of the Warners' driveway and disappeared behind the parked SUV. Anne could only see the leash pulled tight, like a long, low clothesline extended from Helen's hand.

"I feel bad that we don't ask her over with the other

neighbours now, but it's awkward now that she's alone. She's the only one of the old group left here."

"We tried, remember?" Mike said. "She sat there like she was made of stone, and the only thing she said was that when the Weekses owned our house, they had more art on the walls. Then she just stared like she could still see it all hanging there, like she was still looking at it." He was holding the coffee pot as if it were the answer to what should be a particularly obvious riddle. "How many stories about the good old days are you willing to listen to, anyway?"

"Maybe if we invited her another time she could bring Miss Roxy as her date," Anne said. "There's a dog that would look great sitting at the table with a napkin tucked under her collar."

Mike laughed—Anne smiled, too.

"I just think we could be making a bigger effort," she said. "I mean, put yourself in her shoes. What if we were the last ones? What if it was just me or you?"

Then, as Anne looked out the window, Helen disappeared behind the car, too.

HELEN GATHERED THE plastic bag inside out over her hand and bent over slowly. It wasn't easy, and she felt, as she often did, as though she might just lose her balance and topple forward face-first into the pavement.

She had never liked this part, the soft feel of it, the too-familiar warmth through the thin plastic against her hand. Roxy had already moved away to the grass verge, muzzle deep in the new grass, pulling at it with her teeth.

"Don't go making yourself sick now," Helen said. "I don't want to be picking that up, too."

Helen held the bag and looked around carefully. Then she folded the top of the bag open, just a little, and, reaching out, rubbed the soiled plastic in under the cup-shaped door handle on the driver's side of the Warners' car.

It was important not to leave too much, she thought. Just a thin streak, out of sight. Just enough, without leaving any obvious, definite sign. Dirt on their hands, with no idea where it came from. Helen looked at Roxy and Roxy looked back—inscrutable, aware, and, Helen thought, somehow disappointed.

"Time to go home, Roxy," she said. "Time to go home."

FAREWELL TOUR

SAM WASN'T SURE HE was in exactly the right place on the beach: it was the right beach, he knew that. He was absolutely certain of that. But it was daylight now, and when they'd been there together, it had been dark. Now, with the families and children, bathing suits and sand buckets, it looked a lot different.

They had been there late at night and the beach had been empty, not even the teenaged bonfire revellers left, so that the thin slight slap of the small waves coming in white on the shore was the only constant sound. A small crest of foam at the front of each wave caught whatever light there was and reflected it back, a thin repeating line on the edge between the dark sand and the dark sky. They'd been walking hand in hand, the sand giving way slowly under their feet with small

attempts at resistance, and then she let go of his hand
and seemed to disappear into the darkness ahead of
him. Except she didn't vanish. Beth stepped sideways
and stopped directly in front of him, just three steps
ahead, something, he realized later, that she must
have planned the whole time. He walked right into her
and, startled in the dark, his hands sought purchase
on what he'd collided with. She'd caught his wrists
quickly and pressed his hands in tightly on her hips,
arching her neck backwards so she could reach his ear
and whisper.

"Just put it in me right here."

She bent forward and held onto her ankles, her dress
shucked up over her ass. He did what he was told, smiling foolishly out into the darkness, feeling everything,
his pants loose and open, feeling things as disparate as
the belt buckle and the top button on his jeans slapping
loosely against his skin, keeping time. Wondering the
whole time if at any moment a spotlight or a headlight
would flash over them from the now-distant parking
lot — knowing that the fear was groundless and yet still
enthralling.

It was over quickly, and Beth almost matter-of-
factly took her panties out of her jacket pocket and
stepped into them: he was slightly ahead of her, and
watched her silhouetted against the single street light
far down the beach at the parking lot. He had no idea

when she had taken them off, and, distracted, he tried to figure out what he'd been doing so that he hadn't noticed.

WITH A START, Sam realized how completely he had sunk into the memory, standing stock-still in the sand—it was like night had been instantly replaced by day. The sun was beating down, the beach was crowded with fifty or sixty people, the wave-swept sand almost completely marked up with criss-crossing footprints. And Beth? Probably surprising someone else now, he thought.

It had all ended in a rush—Sam couldn't even figure out what the cause was, in fact, if there even was anything as distinct as a cause. There was no building to an angry crescendo—just a gradual winding-down, like a clock losing the energy to flick its second hand even one more space.

"We just seem to have, I don't know, settled down," she'd said. "And I don't like settling."

Three days later, virtually every trace of her was gone from their apartment, like she'd spent a couple of weeks taking inventory and splitting things up. He half expected to pick up something as simple as a mug, turn it over, and find a square of masking tape with "Sam's" written on it in her handwriting. What she had done was more than just leaving: it was like a surgical strike, well planned and carefully executed.

She had erased herself, he thought, from absolutely everything but his memory. Not long after she left, he wished she had stripped herself out of there as well.

Sam was never ready when some memory of her returned. He'd decide to make potato salad, and be shaken by an unexpected image of Beth at the counter, cutting cooked potatoes into cubes. The way her smile gathered at the corners of her mouth, the rise and fall, shoulder to hip, when she was facing away from him in bed and tented lightly under a single sheet. He'd remembered holding her when they were picking blueberries, both of them sweaty, while she insisted she was able to suck the blue stain from his fingers, and he twisted with desire from the feeling of her tongue against his fingertips. Familiar places were like a minefield, but the nighttime was worse. Sam lost count of the times he dreamt about finding Beth in the places they'd gone on vacation: the cottage in Nova Scotia's Annapolis Valley, the Prince Edward Island old-style resort with the long beach directly across the road, the Mexican town where they had a small separate suite with a balcony looking out and down over an ancient-looking market.

He'd explained it to his friends at work, who seemed to be decidedly sick of the whole topic of Beth and her sudden departure.

"It's like I have to undo the things we did," he told them. "I've got enough saved up to go to every single place we ever went together, and enough vacation time on the books to do it all at the one time." He told Mitch and Kevin, both rushing through their coffees, that he thought the best thing to do was to overwrite all the memories of being a couple with new experiences, so that if he had to travel in his sleep, he could at least travel by himself.

"She's sewn right into me in all of those places," he said. "I'm going to take the stitches out."

Mitch told him that he thought the idea was stupid. Kevin was a little more gracious: "You've got to do something," he said, but it sounded a little more grudging than Sam would have liked.

Sam went to Mexico first, and right away, while still on the plane, he wondered if both his friends hadn't been right: he had to do something, but perhaps the trip was a stupid idea. He hadn't gotten much further than the idea that he would go to each place. Perhaps, he thought, he should have spent more time planning what he would do when he actually got there. He'd successfully booked the same suite in the small Mexican town they'd visited, but he hadn't expected what it would be like on the first morning there. Exhausted from the trip, he'd fallen into a turbulent and fractured sleep, his first waking thought while standing by the mirror that Beth's hairbrush was missing from the spot where it should have been, where it had been, two full years before.

He made coffee and drank it all, the whole pot, sitting at the same wrought-iron table he'd sat at all those months earlier, his cup rocking every time he set it down on the floral pattern twisted into the metal. It was a familiar teeter—he knew the cup couldn't topple, but he kept reaching for it after he set it down, his hand coming forward every time the cup wobbled.

When he visited the market in town, it only reminded him about how concerned he'd been when Beth had found a stall selling freshly squeezed orange juice and bought a plastic glass full.

"Aren't you worried about getting sick?" he'd asked. "Montezuma's revenge and all that?"

"Aren't you going to lighten up and live a little?" she had laughed back at him. It seemed like banter then— in retrospect, he thought, more like judgment.

He counted familiar things off on his fingers as he passed them: the pastry shop where they'd bought water and a handful of almond-flavoured cookies for breakfast; a restaurant where they'd skipped having a meal and settled on repeated vodka and sodas for her and dark beers for him; a huge open-air place with a handful of mid-afternoon customers where she'd suggested they should head for the bathroom together—"It'll be worth your while"—but had settled on reaching under the table and putting her hand high up on his thigh, tucked beneath the edge of his shorts, looking at him mischievously and giving his leg a squeeze. Behind her, he caught a table of three men snatching looks at her, in between a loose discussion about the costs and benefits of surface mining. There was the store where she'd bought an incredibly form-fitting long jersey dress, cream-coloured, in which she spontaneously developed a habit of regularly pushing her hands down her sides, pulling the cloth tantalizingly close to her skin every time. He hadn't told her she was doing it, but he found himself almost waiting for her palms to begin their downward and figure-defining travel.

This is not working at all, he thought later that night, lying in the same bed they'd shared, looking at the same gently spinning ceiling fan.

He fell asleep with the lights on and woke up in the middle of the night confused, displaced, and shaking from the memory of her laughter ringing through the room. Her laughter, he thought. Throaty. Full of trouble. And now, surrounding him.

I have three more days booked before flying to Nova Scotia, he thought the next morning, looking down glumly at the same green chili breakfast enchilada that Beth had ordered almost every day they'd been there.

On the second night, a Friday, he resolutely tried to spend his way through a fistful of hundred-peso notes at a dark but busy side-street bar, a place he and Beth had passed every single day walking through the town, gripping his beer tightly and telling himself that he was having fun. Halfway through the evening, a woman sat down next to him and smiled, and Sam liked that, until they struggled through the language barrier and both established that she expected to be paid. He had smiled ruefully, offered a flat "No, *gracias*," and almost changed his mind as he watched her walk away.

He threw up on the uneven cobblestones on his way back to the hotel, beer and foam cutting in angled runnels between the stones. He had to lean on the wall after he rang the bell and waited, embarrassed, for the security guard to open the metal gate and let him in.

Sam spent the entire next day in the room, the curtains drawn, trying to keep his eyes closed, the "Do not disturb" sign on his door not only because he was hungover, but because he simply didn't want to look out and see the town anymore.

On what was supposed to be his last day in the town, he checked out early and hired a car to take him back to Mexico City, where he stayed the night in a featureless hotel near the airport that held the singular benefit that he and Beth had never been near the place.

Nova Scotia was a different kind of pain. He had forgotten that their trip to the Annapolis Valley had been one of their very first together. When he had planned his return trip, he'd carefully booked the same cabin, only to realize when he pulled up in the rental car that he had conveniently forgotten that the place was almost without any sort of distraction, that their main experience of the place was mostly under the covers and inside the walls, which were themselves remarkably stark.

The cabin was near the Gaspereau River, settled into the side of a hill with regimented rows of apple trees in front of it. Inside, Sam saw—and remembered—the picture of a farmer boy in overalls standing next to two aproned girls on the living room wall, a pullout couch that must have been bought cheap, because its crushed green velvet and floral pattern was too garish for anyone to buy for their home. There were four galley chairs around a small dining table covered with a plastic tablecloth decorated with pictures of grapes, strawberries, and pears, a design that absorbed any possible surface stain as just another piece of its complicated pattern.

The cabin was so plain, he thought, so empty of personality that Beth's absence was as obvious as if he'd gone into the tiny bathroom and noticed in the bathroom mirror that one of his front teeth was suddenly missing. He had never been anywhere, he realized, where her presence had been so totally part of the room.

There were two other cottages in the row—both empty—and an absolutely traditional white farm-house where the owners lived. They told him to make himself at home—that they were heading to Halifax to hit the shopping centres and bulk stores for supplies for the upcoming tourist season.

"You're our first guest this year," the woman said. "I'm sorry we're not better prepared. We don't usually see anyone this early."

She gave him three days' worth of towels, all smell-ing strongly of fabric softener, four hand soaps, and two extra rolls of toilet paper before they left. Sam had a feeling that she recognized him, and guessed why he was alone. And that she felt sorry for him.

He realized later that night that the owners had turned off every light in the house before they left, so Sam's cabin was a barren little pool of empty light all by itself in a mostly darkened valley, with only the stars and a line of street lights along a distant ridge to break the almost-absolute darkness. When he went outside, there were so many stars in the sky that it seemed almost oppressive, as if the sky was actually bulging down toward him, pressing all those stars closer. Like he was being forced to eat.

Beth, it seemed to Sam, would be impossible to avoid.

But he tried anyway.

He found his way back out past Port Williams—to the great long fine-sand-and-mud beaches drained by the Bay of Fundy's tides—and promptly remembered that Beth had lost her watch on the same beach when she had left it safely on a rock well above the water's edge. The tide raced in over the flats faster than they had imagined, even though the strength and speed of the tides was almost always part of any tourism advertisement.

He'd been upset: Beth had laughed. "It's my own fault," she'd said, as if that meant she wasn't allowed to be upset about it. He drove the same back roads, stopped and had chowder at the same place that had disappointed him before, the chowder milky and thin, the clams scarce.

He went into Wolfville and walked the sea dykes and the barely used railway tracks. Drove to the same beach where the wind had turned cold, but where they'd lain on their stomachs and searched the beach gravel for rose quartz and agates. Stretched out with their feet at opposite compass points, they were face to face, picking through the same small field of stones, and all he had to do was look up to watch her searching the beach in front of her. The expression on her face was one that she had when she was truly concentrating. The way Sam remembered it, she caught him looking

at her a couple of times, and smiled quickly before looking back at the beach stones.

Coming back down the valley toward the cabin,
Sam also stopped just below a hydroelectric plant,
where the river turned in a dark and slow circle, the
powerful current bulging up occasionally to the surface like loosely molded jelly, before the water turned
downstream toward the sea.

They hadn't been there together, but Sam remembered catching sight of the dark water as they passed in
the car from somewhere else. He would have liked to
stop then, but it was something that he had thought she
might not have enjoyed—when she had been in the car
with him, he'd simply kept driving.

Sitting next to the water—looking across at the
"No Swimming" signs complete with skull and cross-
bones—was better than rattling around inside the
walls of the cabin, he thought.

Sam was strangely hopeful when he handed back
the cabin keys and started the drive to Prince Edward
Island. He wasn't sure if it was because the cure was
working, or simply because the trip was almost over.
The car had satellite radio, a station that played songs
he hadn't heard before, but that seemed to be the kind
of music he could quickly like. Maybe the thing is to
focus on the differences, he thought: look sharply at
them, and then let your eyes drift.

But Sam hadn't been prepared for the beach.

One moment he was walking in the sand, feeling the heat of the sun battering against his skin while it reflected off the surface of the water, the noise of children and families and passing boats full in his ears. The next, it was silent, except for the quiet lop of the small waves falling over themselves on the sandy shore, and it was dark, and he could sense her out there in front of him, feel the warmth and shape of her, the kind of sixth sense that sometimes makes you slow down for no reason before you actually meet an obstacle. Sam hit the solid, soft wall of Beth's memory hard, even as he realized she wasn't there at all.

He was amazed to find himself back in the front seat of his rental car, unable to remember staggering his way back across the soft beach sand, not knowing if he had pushed through sandcastles or across moats and over beach blankets, wondering if he had left a wake of startled children and angry parents behind him.

He was able to get himself together enough to start the car and head back to the hotel, making the shallow curves on the road almost by rote, his mind elsewhere.

The resort had been a rail baron's island getaway — broken up now into suites, bathrooms added wherever necessary and possible — but it was still very much an old estate, tightly packed with wooden features and stuffed animal heads, every downstairs room remarkably suited to deep chairs and the slow ticking of clocks. It even had a billiards room, although the whole time he was there, no one played.

The resort was also renowned for its dinner service. Beth had read that word to him when she'd booked the place, "re-now-n-ed," like it had four formal and full syllables. Maybe too renowned.

"You're in the first sitting? We're overbooked."

The woman at the front desk wasn't apologetic in the least. A small, sharp-looking woman in a dark jacket, she said the words as if she was throwing them straight at him, almost daring him to react.

"I'm sorry?" Sam said.

"Too many people, too few tables." She made it sound like she was talking to someone who was slightly, but obviously, slow. "You'll have to share."

"Share?"

"Yes. Share. There will be someone else at your table."

Sam wasn't sure he was ready to talk to anyone over dinner. He thought about staying in his room, but remembered all at once that it was wallpapered with Beth. At least, it was wallpapered with a paper that Beth had thought was hilarious when they'd been there, an expensive, formal-looking gold-and-red-wine-flocked repeating pattern of a knight on a horse, his helmet on, lance pointed resolutely toward the ground. She had been hopelessly reduced to giggles at the sight of it. "It should say 'the can't-get-it-up suite' right on the door. Who the hell would pick something like that?" She laughed.

It hadn't been anything of the sort back then, Sam thought humourlessly, but it would be now.

He pictured having dinner with an elderly man travelling on business, a group of insurance brokers, a couple with a small and food-throwing child. Any one of them would be better, he thought, than a long and hungry night surrounded by Beth and the knights of the limp lance.

When he came downstairs, though, the waiter led him through the dining room and out into the windowed veranda that surrounded two sides of the building, each holding rows of single tables.

The waiter stopped at a table where a woman was already sitting.

"I ..." Sam started, turning toward a waiter who was already pulling a chair out for him. Then he stopped.

"I'm Peggy," the woman said. She was tanned, with very white teeth. He could tell because she was smiling. A small woman, at least, smaller than Beth, wearing a sleeveless light top that showed off strong shoulders.

He sat down. "I'm Sam."

Sam thought that he could beat her to the punch, ask first before she got around to asking why a single guy was at a place packed with couples and families.

"I'm exorcising demons," she answered, making a strange, almost feathery motion with her fingers, her hand turned backwards toward the rest of the room, held up over her shoulder. "Well, not really. We were supposed to get married here."

She looked across at Sam, at the expression on his face.

"No, I mean my fiancé and I. We had the place booked and everything. I did it all online: banquet services, the dessert options, the menus. Date picked and deposit made. I could only get the deposit back as a credit note." She looked at the glass as if she were seeing something different. "I guess I wanted to see what it was like in real life, in case I didn't ever get the chance again."

Drinks arrived, and, fascinated, Sam found himself asking what happened.

"Things didn't work out. Kind of suddenly, really."

"I know what that's like," Sam said.

Then he explained why he was there, and Peggy seemed to understand the idea much better than either Mitch or Kevin had. It even seemed to make sense to her.

"I have a friend who does that all the time with guitar players," she said, smiling again. "When she breaks up with one, she just goes out with another. Except I'm not sure she actually plans it that way."

Sam felt his face breaking into a smile, realizing that,

for months, he'd become unaccustomed to smiling.

Peggy had scallops—Sam splurged and had the lobster. He even wore the silly plastic bib and didn't worry about the mess or about the fact the menu said only "market price." An hour and a half later, they were still talking, and separate checks eventually came without prompting, the waiter placing the two folders on the edge of the table and drifting out of sight. Outside, the sky had lighted to orange with the sunset, then faded into purple.

"What are you doing tomorrow?" Sam asked, bold and slightly red-cheeked after three glasses of the house wine.

"I thought I might go for a walk on the beach. Want to come along?"

The words felt like a hammer on tin, and Sam waited for the inevitable arrival of Beth—and waited. Then waited a little more. He saw Peggy looking at him across the table, curious.

"I'd love to," he replied.

They had dinner together after spending the day together, and then did the same the next day, the same table each time. Sam found himself wishing he hadn't bothered travelling anywhere else, wishing that he had more time.

It had only been a few days, but Sam could already draw up Peggy's face in his head with his eyes closed, the slope of her cheekbones, even the way her hands flew around when she was talking excitedly.

The third night, they both had lobster, both wearing the bibs, neither one embarrassed by the way they looked. They were still in the restaurant after everyone else had left, the wait staff changing the other tables over for breakfast.

Peggy reached across the table and took just the tips of his fingers in her hand. He felt an electric surge running through his arm, a hollow, eager ache.

"This has been just great," she said.

It was a feeling that he doubted he would ever be able to forget.

THREE DAYS

ARTHUR SIMMONS THOUGHT ABOUT just staying put this time and urinating in the bed. Wondered if that would be going too far.

He'd been in bed for two full days already. This morning would mark the third morning that no one had come, and no one had even called to check on him.

He looked over at the phone, a flat 1970s push-button, cream-coloured, silent, sitting on the table beside the bed. It wouldn't take much effort to call, he thought, neither for me nor for them. But he had resisted. Art was following the rules he'd set for himself from the very beginning: wait. Wait for someone else to make the first move. Wait, for as long as it took.

He was taking short, shallow breaths, aware that breathing more deeply would start another round of coughing. He'd heard somewhere that, once you got old, you could easily cough hard enough to crack a rib, and he believed it. Every time the coughing started, he felt like an old bellows with its handles being pumped too hard: air rushing out, rattling back in again, shaking things loose and starting the whole cycle all over again. Each coughing spell was exhausting, and afterwards, he would feel as if he was unable to lift his arms. He stayed as still as he could, breathing flatly through his nose. It had started as a cold on Sunday. By Monday, he could feel the weight of it shifting into his chest, settling there, and he knew he was really sick, the kind of illness that is more a forced march than a nuisance.

It was five o'clock on a late June morning, a Thursday, and there had already been light outside at four-thirty—he could see it edging in through the blinds in thin stripes, the night lightening to a pale grey.

Would wetting the bed make the point any more clearly? Would it make them pay any more attention if they ever got around to finding him?

He imagined the feel of brief, welcome warmth, while the rest of the day would be clammy, the room filled with the particularly sharp stink of old man's urine.

ARTHUR WOULD GET up to go to the bathroom, but that was the only time he'd been getting up, shuffling slowly down the hall, and stopping to lean against the wall when the coughing overtook him. He would stop afterwards to get a drink of water from the sink and, at the same time, hate himself for that small weakness. But that was it, the only times he'd move from the bed. He hadn't been downstairs to the kitchen, hadn't picked up the phone to call anyone. Outside, there might well be mail waiting for him in the mailbox, a handful of flyers and one or two bills. They could stay there, he thought. He wanted every hour to count, each minute on the clock to be a precise measure of guilt.

There had been six others in his family, three brothers, three sisters, but they had all died. All their wives and husbands were gone, too. A dead generation. Was that too harsh? Should he be thinking they've "passed"? Or maybe that Salvation Army saying, "promoted to Glory?"

But they weren't promoted to anywhere, he thought. They'd just winked out, there one day, packed up and gone the next. Perhaps it would be closer to say they were fired into purgatory.

It was a thought he kept coming back to: the fact that everything they had been, everything they had done, was just gone, too. He was it: the last, the final custodian, the keeper of all the information. Memories?

Facts? Experience? All gone, he thought. All wasted. Trapped in the last remaining memories of someone who couldn't even find anyone who cared enough to stop and listen.

There wasn't any prize for being the survivor, Art thought. But he didn't miss his siblings, not any of them. Not Anne with her ability to go stomping off righteously after the slightest provocation, her chin firmly in the air and ready to hold onto the slight for years. Nor Heather, whose skill at winning any argument had left the rest of her siblings unwilling to talk to her about any important topic, let alone engage in debate. But he did miss the things they'd done together. Summers in Maine, for example, sailing small boats on the Eggemoggin Reach near Mount Desert Island. Rowing to any one of the small, empty islands along the reach to dig through ancient shell middens for arrowhead fragments or wandering the beaches collecting sand dollars.

Art could remember heading out through the roiling tidal currents with his mother in the family canoe, his brother Mark in the middle, Art in the bow, pulling hard past one of the big houses on the shore, a Rockefeller relative or something with a great barn of a boathouse down on the shore, a seaplane nestled up at the top of the boathouse ramp like a stiff-winged bird waiting to be startled into instant motion, into uncatchable escape. Art could remember his mother saying that the salt water was riskier canoeing, but better for the canoe, especially in the several places where beaching the craft had chipped the dark green paint away. "Salt water won't help," she had said, "but it won't rot the canvas, either." He could remember the taste of that salt, too, licking it off the back of his hand, his left hand, the hand that most often took the bottom grip on the canoe paddle. He remembered the day as being dark, glowering, the water particularly choppy. But all his reference points were gone: his mother, dead twenty years now, and Mark buried six years later after four long months of cancer fingering ungently through his bones.

There was no one left to ask about it, Art thought. Realizing—again—that his version of the experience was now the truth. It could have been sunny that day, he thought. I could have gotten it wrong. His mother might only have told him about the seaplane. The doors to the boathouse might have been tightly closed, the rest of it he might've made up in his head. It might not have been the Rockefellers at all, although he knew for certain they'd had summer homes there.

Arthur did get things wrong sometimes: several times, years earlier, he'd told his brothers and sisters about something he remembered, only to be met with blank stares, incomprehension.

"You have the most vivid imagination." That would
have to have been Eleanor, who, if nothing else, was
always certain that her version was absolutely, impec-
cably right.

Now, Art thought, she would have been the right
one to be the survivor—but she'd gone, and left quick,
too. One morning, she'd called a nearby friend, another
retired and widowed woman who'd arrived in a rush to
find every single coffee maker in the house taken apart
and laid out on the counter—glass percolator, French
press, filter drip. Every piece, laid out in order like a
mechanic's tear-down manual, as if she were trying to
figure out just exactly how each of them worked. It was
a startling combination of scientific rigour and absolute
bewilderment.

"All I want is a cup of coffee," the normally prim
Ellie had told her friend. "And I don't care what the fuck
you have to do to make it."

Two months later, she was dead, too, also cancer,
tumours cropping up in her brain and everywhere else
like weeds filtering up through a lawn, travelling along
unseen, unmarked tangles of underground roots.

"It wasn't anywhere until it was everywhere," her
doctor told Art on the phone, at the same time managing to make it sound like the doctor felt he had been the
victim of a particularly horrible magic trick. Eleanor
had no kids: her executor was her family lawyer,

who sent Art his sister's ashes in a plain brown-paper-wrapped package.

Second last to go was John. Art and John stopped even sending Christmas cards after Ellie's death. Art had never seen the point in the first place, and with John, it was as if hearing about Eleanor's ashes ending up with Art was the last straw.

"You're not the oldest," John protested in one last distant and tinny-sounding bitter phone call. "You're not even the oldest one left."

At that moment, Art suddenly found himself wanting to remind John that, when they had shared a room during the family's summers in Maine, John had always been the one who had been frightened by the big summer thunderstorms coursing up the reach. So scared in fact that one night, in the middle of a heavy storm poised almost directly overhead, Art had woken up to find that John had climbed into his bed, so that, rolling over, Art could see the whites of John's wide-open eyes with every flare of lightning.

Reminding John of that over the phone had seemed like the best response, but at the same time, it was something held out of bounds by unwritten family rules. There were things they all knew, but just never said.

Like the fact that their brother Mark had been, for the briefest of periods, a bedwetter. Everyone in the

family had one or more memories of their mother hauling great bundles of sheets and blankets out of Mark's
room in the middle of the night, an event that always
seemed overlarge and overwrought by the rush and
the fact it always occurred around two or three in the
morning. Mark, as always, managing to be the centre
of attention again.

John had dodged all the big threats: cancer and heart
disease and stroke had all kept their distance, islands of
cholesterol had no doubt floated benignly through his
veins without ever successfully blocking anything. In
his seventies, though, John had stepped on the upturned
tines of a rock rake while gardening. He became living—and eventually dying—proof of the difficulty of
cleansing deep puncture wounds and had died of blood
poisoning after a full week in hospital.

John had kids—three of them, but only two were in
the country to sit next to his bed as the infection grew,
making his foot enormous and multicoloured, draining
horribly, and then growing massive again. As he moved
in and out of consciousness, the two adult children
made careful and quiet funeral plans at his bedside
while the third, a son, wrestled with airline schedules
and business commitments and managed to get back
just before John slipped into a final coma. John's first
and last words to his travelling son? "You've put on a
bit of weight."

Ellie had no children—Anne and Mark had two, Heather one, Ian and John both had three.

Art had two children as well, a boy and a girl. In total, he calculated, everyone's children came out to one short of the total number of parents, a family destined to be in slow decline.

Maybe it's pneumonia, Art thought, feeling the gentle rattle in his chest every time he breathed. The default killer of scores of the elderly, up there with congestive heart failure on a scorecard of the most likely causes. His brother Ian had soldiered on through multiple sclerosis and skin cancer and the loss of both a kidney and a lung—with his shirt off, the scars looked as though he had been inexpertly repaired by amateurs— but it was pneumonia that had finally won the battle.

At the end, Ian had become a fiery wraith of himself, a leathery leftover puppet strung together with sinew and tendons that looked more and more like fat, braided rope as everything else melted away. Art had gone to visit him, the last time with Ian bending up toward him urgently from his hospital bed as if he had something critical to impart, eyes wide and intense.

"You win," he finally managed to say, and Art was pretty certain that Ian was smiling when he said it. It was hard to tell: Ian's face was pulled tight by that time, stretched over his skull as if it were drying on a board for taxidermy. But Art was convinced from the sound of his voice that the smile was real. Ian died a day later, stopping breathing only when it seemed that everything left of his body had already consumed itself to ash.

Arthur noticed the light behind the blinds had brightened, hardened.

It would have been nice to open the blinds, maybe even open the bedroom window, too, Art thought. See a bit of the sun. Get a little fresh air in: Art wasn't sure, but he had a feeling that the room might smell bad—stale, or even worse. You get used to something and it's just normal, he thought. But every now and then, he'd catch a hint of a smell of something off—the kind of smell that would then flit away from his senses, as if concentrating on it only served to make it more discreet. Either way, it wouldn't hurt to air the place out, he thought.

But that would mean getting up and, in the process, losing the high ground. First I'd be opening the windows, then I'd be creeping downstairs to make a sandwich, he thought. Then the whole effort would be lost. Hunger's a funny thing, Art thought. He had been hungry, but the feeling had faded. Now, he wasn't sure that he would be able to eat even if he tried.

Instead, Art lay on his back in bed in the half-light of the room, watching the dust dance in one thin band of sunlight that was coming through a hall window and reaching all the way through the door into his bedroom. There were only a handful of days, he thought, on either side of the summer solstice when the sun was in the right place to actually make the straight line and reach the room. He'd noticed it before: the same kind of strange, poignant, meaningless marker as when, all too frequently it seemed, he'd glance at a clock and see the digital numbers all line up: 11:11.

He wondered who would be the first to call, or the first to show up.

Would it be Patrick or Jane? They'd both become more and more uninterested as the years had gone by: Patrick, busy enough with a family of his own, and Jane, a health care consultant, on the road more often than not.

A week ago, Jane had read him the riot act when he'd asked her to help him get groceries. "Honestly, Dad, I can't be at your beck and call. I'm not even in the province half the time. We've got to find a better way."

Five years ago, she would never have said that. Five years ago, he thought, she would have gotten the groceries herself, brought them over, helped him with supper, and they would have eaten together, cleaning the kitchen with an easy hand-off of the tasks between them.

He wasn't sure what time it was now. The clock on the bureau was slightly turned away, and he couldn't

see the numbers clearly or reach it without getting out
of bed. Art decided it must be close to ten.

By then, he'd practised his first sentence several
times, listened to it rattle around his bedroom when he
said it out loud, astounded by how thin and reedy his
voice sounded.

"I haven't been out of bed in three days."

No, not quite.

"I haven't been strong enough to even get out of this
bed for three days."

That was better—if that didn't make them stop
and take notice, he didn't know what would. Maybe
he could act drowsy and a bit confused when someone
finally came upstairs. And he could muster up a deep,
rattling cough with no problem. When he thought
about coughing, he could feel the fluttering in his
lungs, a cough that wanted to start, and he managed to
hold the reflex at bay until it faded away.

As the urge to cough faded, a memory rose, flickering like an old film: Patrick and Jane, both still children, somewhere between five and ten, in their aunt
Anne's yard in Maine, during a summer when Anne
had been breeding setter puppies. He remembered
bright sunshine, the clumsy new puppies tumbling
and rolling over in the grass, Jane on her then-pudgy
knees with her hands held straight up over her head
in the air, Patrick holding a puppy carefully while the

dog chewed busily on his thumb with its new, needling teeth. Both Anne and the puppies' mother carefully attentive, not interfering but clearly concentrating on everything that was happening. Tolerantly on guard. Anne had already explained that the mother dog—was its name Dex? Art couldn't be sure—might nip if she felt her puppies were in danger. Both children smiling, concentrating on the small dogs. The kind of memory Art could hold in his mind and see as sharply as if he were holding a photograph of it in his hands.

It's all in here, Art thought, one hand behind his head as if he could safely cradle every thought. All of it. He was watching the light behind the venetian blinds changing.

All they had to do was ask.

Afternoon came.

Then evening.

Three days folded gently into four.

Art slept.

HEAVY LOAD

WE'RE GOING TO TRUNDLE eighty tons over that over-pass with the concrete side rails, two inches to spare on either side, *two inches*, and everybody had better have gotten their measurements right, because if someone's measuring tape slipped and they didn't go back and measure it again, we're going to be stuck in there like a cork in a bottle and there's going to be hell to pay.

And I'm the only one who's going to be there for the whole ride. The other project engineers come into the office real bright and chipper and ready for their first coffee in the morning, then they're out the door at five, home and then straight to bed in the evening after watching *Dancing With the Stars* or whatever. And they've got no idea we've worked right through the night, sixteen hours straight, and we're still out there

the whole time they're sleeping. That we've been creeping along with the multi-wheeler and the hard hats and
eighty tons of module for the project, eight hours overnight to get the haul done with the road closed—main
route, straight to downtown—with cops sitting there
with their lights flashing, stopping traffic, wishing they
were anywhere else than babysitting us.

The whole parade moves at two miles an hour, fourteen miles to cover in all, a little extra time because
something always goes wrong and that's why I'm there,
to make decisions instead of having everybody just
argue back and forth and waste time. Expensive time.

They built the module in a fabricating yard out by
the highway, at an industrial park with all the electrical
lines buried, so at least I don't have to worry about a
mess overhead, just on the road. It's going from there
to the waterfront and then onto an offshore supply boat
and out to the oil fields, but I don't have anything to do
with that part. I just have to get the module safely to
the wharf. It doesn't really matter what it's for, that's
not my worry, but I know that it's an oil/water sep-
arator, just like I always want to know what it is. Not
that it would matter to anyone else—but it does to me.
It's a great big thing, pipes jutting out from it everywhere, and it's painted bright yellow and bright blue
and orange like the industry's just suddenly discovered
this thing called colour.

I'll go with it the whole way, yard to wharf, not because anyone told me I have to, but because that's the way you get something done.

You get things done by doing them yourself. And that's what those new kids don't understand.

I've picked up parts at the airport from Learjet pilots who just flew them in, driving right out to meet the plane on the back side of the airport, the box still warm from the factory—still warm—and I had them on site and out into assembly before anyone else had even had their morning coffee. And when I did, I was the one on the phone, yelling, the day before, "Yes, you are going to fly them out because you made a commitment and we have a schedule, and if they're not here by six a.m., you'll be paying every cent of the penalty clause."

They were "Yes sir, yes, Mr. Campbell, it will be there."

And I said, "You get it here like you're supposed to, and you can even call me Robert." Because I don't miss deadlines, not even one. I never have, and I'm not about to start now. I'll get it done on time if I have to pull the trailer in by myself. With my teeth.

Every year, we get a couple more interns, engineering students in their last year, and they all think exactly the same way, that you can manage a project or a move sitting in your car, or, better yet, from the comfort of your chair at the nine-to-five office, spitting out long-distance orders that just get followed, sure that everything will go right. Not understanding for a moment the consequences of the whole damn thing going wrong. Not even thinking it could go wrong. People say old ways die hard, but these new guys think they're all white-collar guys and they think the white-collar guys stay in the office while the blue-collars do the grunt work.

Maybe by the end of the three months or six months they have with us, they'll have learned a thing or two, like the fact that eighty-ton modules don't spin around the room on the coasters under your office chair.

That's why I find myself working right through.

In the middle of the night—not midnight or even one a.m., but the real night, well after two and closing in on three or even later, when even the drunks go quiet. The trees are absolutely still, the only sound the grumble of the big machines sitting and waiting to start moving, the only light the shine of the flashlights and running lights and headlights from the reflective lines on the safety vests. Men moving quietly, without instructions, like they do on the docks, shifting lines as the ships bend and knuckle out into the dark of the harbour. There's a purposeful preparation in it, everyone ready and moving in a pattern, as choreographed as a dance, each person doing their own part of the checklist before we do anything else. Unconnected, but in concert.

We move out like the slowest kind of parade, with not a soul there to watch us, the night so still that you can actually hear the lenses of the warning lights spinning inside their clear orange plastic covers, the big "Wide Load" sign tied on the back even though the road's closed and no one's going to see it anyway, because that's exactly what the regulations say you have to do. You hear the big engine bend into the job: you actually do, you hear it lean forward and pull every bit as much as if it were a team of horses putting their shoulders down into the traces. It's not like that with a car, but with a big-cycle diesel, that's different. The sound of it drops low, powerful, torque introducing itself to inertia.

For a moment, nothing happens. Nothing moves.

And then, it does. You can watch the wheels and imagine that there's no way they will ever turn, and then there is that first slight shift, so small you almost wonder if your eyes have got it wrong. From motionless to motion, just like that. Slow at first, speeding up really gradually. And everybody starts to walk, keeping pace.

Flashing lights catch in the trees the most, playing across all those trunks and branches, especially on the highway. There's the repetition of them in every one of the bright Xs of the safety vests. Orange lights from the hauler and the trailer, red and blue and white from the police cars until they get tired of the whole thing and drop back. The first thing you'd think, coming up on us, is that something momentous, something tragic has happened in the night. But absolutely the last thing we're looking for is excitement—we spend the whole quiet, slowly moving night hoping that nothing happens at all.

We've got the eastbound lane all to ourselves, and the whole highway's different when you're only creeping along. You sweep along the road at a hundred kilometres an hour—never stopping to think about how much work is built right into it. Walking, you can feel the summer heat battering back up at you from the pavement, surrendering slowly back into the night air. You can feel the heat coming up around you in waves, the way you might see it shimmering as you looked across the length of a parking lot.

For the first two miles, it's a series of gentle bends, a long swing to the left, and then two overpasses. On the bends, you can feel the road sloping down under your feet, feel just that little bit of banking that manages to keep a handful of speeders from crashing, despite themselves, every year. This road's fifteen years old, and I can't help but think you could get down on your hands and knees and measure, and the angle of the banking would still be bang on the mark, not a single driver the wiser, probably not one in a hundred who even knows it's there. But it's my job to control everything—to know every single thing before it even has a chance to happen. The inclinometer on the trailer is reading six degrees, but that's no surprise, because that's what the highways department told us the incline would be. I called a guy I know with the road builders too, and he told me that we wouldn't hit anything steeper than that, which is nowhere near steep enough for anything to slide sideways, for the load to overcome inertia's steady grip.

I KNOW ABOUT inertia's grip. For forty years, Bev and I had the same breakfast: two eggs over easy with whole wheat toast for me while Bev had oatmeal and fruit. We married when we were in our twenties and had three kids, almost exactly two years apart every time. Both of us at that kitchen table every morning while the kids grew up, went to school, and finally moved out. Breakfast was the time when we had a chance to talk about the kids until one day when they weren't there anymore and there wasn't anything left to talk about. Eventually, we just sat and ate our breakfast with only the sounds of forks and spoons randomly ringing off plates and bowls. I'm torn over whether it was a sign that we'd succeeded at raising kids or failed horribly at something else.

I mean, things wind down. Nobody would expect that we'd be like teenagers once we found ourselves in an empty house. I'm older—she's older. She's not the beauty she once was, though she's still beautiful. I'm not the guy I used to be, either. It's only natural that some things would fade, that I wouldn't be as interested as I was. Natural or not, that was the sticking point for her.

I still don't think it was a bad suggestion—maybe I could have put it better. It wasn't like I was drawing up a flow chart or something. What I said was that, when you look at the week, Monday and Tuesday are the busiest, and all things considered, maybe the best thing we could do was to just plan for Thursday nights.

Bev shouted at me: "You can't just calculate everything, no matter how hard you want to."

But you can—you can calculate anything. You just have to know what all the variables are. Bev shouted, loud enough to be heard outside, for Christ's sake, that she wanted to be "desired, not pencilled in."

All I wanted to say to her was that we should calm down, that we've each got a job to do. We know what our jobs are. Stay focused on the task at hand. We can work our way through this rationally.

But she didn't want to listen. And the whole load was starting to slide.

WHEN WE CAME to the first highway overpass with the module, we slowed down even more. Expansion joints may just be another piece of everyday highway engineering, but we've got to get over them real slow and onto the bridge deck proper as gently as we can. Ever been stopped on a bridge and had a dump truck go by fast? Felt the ground jump? The heavier the load, the bigger difference even a little speed makes. Higher bounces, bigger flex. So we crawl over, stop, and check everything on the other side and use the slope to start us going again.

Along that stretch, there are houses on both sides, tucked in behind earth berms and a noise wall, all we can see from the road are the different-coloured roof shingles and the occasional top few courses of siding. There's not a window in sight, like each house realizes that it's something to be ashamed of, and is ignoring whatever's happening out here.

Sometimes, sound is your best friend. Right away on the downhill, there's a metallic ping like something under tension or maybe a strand of cable's let go, so I shout, "Whoa!" and we crawl all over the module like flies on dessert, checking every tie-down. We're losing time, but we've got a bit of a cushion built in for just this kind of thing.

We don't find anything, but it's a good thing to do in case anyone's attention's flagging.

I can hear everything. A quiet night, no wind, and I hear a police car or a fire truck in the distance, the siren rising and falling. A couple of motorcycle engines, blatting flatly, the sound stuttering and clipped by the summer air. Once, someone shouting, so far away that his words were indistinct, but close enough to know it was a guy. If it had been June, I know that by now we would have been hearing the first birds of the morning, a few chirps and warbles from the early risers when the horizon's just starting to get an almost greyish-white band. But this is the first week of August, so it's still solid dark.

Soon, we'll be on the last big uphill before the narrowest part, the most challenging part, the curving overpass with the long concrete wall. There's always been a shipyard there and they put up the wall to keep some yo-yo in a car from flinging an empty beer bottle over the side and having it fall forty feet down and smack some riveter in the side of the face. It's that wall that makes the overpass so narrow. It's too big to take down, and there just isn't any other way to get around.

The wall's not going to be a problem for us for another hour or so because the hill we've got to climb first is the steepest yet. The hill is the biggest variable, the one point on the trip that I had to factor into all the loading. The hauler's down in its lowest gear and it's blowing black smoke with the effort, the engine making a kind of deep-set humming that I can feel between my teeth. It's going flat out and time is running away on us, because we're not making any speed at all. I try to look at my watch only when everyone else is busy doing something else: if they think we're behind, I worry they'll start to rush and let something slip. I'd rather have time penalties, rather eat shit from the city for missing our time window, than have the module slip off the side of the rig or something. Rushing too much could mean we'd end up caught there for a day or more while we try to figure out the safest way to get the module back on the trailer and squared away. Not to mention trying to figure out if it had been damaged in the fall and what that could cost.

We were right in the middle of the sharpest part of the hill and the whole rig started to lose speed—well, lose whatever scrap of speed it had—and the engine sound wasn't changing and I was just waiting for the whole bottom of the motor to blow right out and spray oil and hydraulic fluid all over the pavement, and boy, if that happened, you'd better get the wheels chocked in a hurry and hope the chocks all hold. I could even see it in my mind's eye: the trailer and the module and the rig all lit up by morning sunshine, everybody underneath packing absorbent sheets into the spilling fluids and waiting for a heavy equipment mechanic to tell us that the whole thing was shot. It isn't the kind of thing that's anyone's fault, but that doesn't really matter, does it?

Finally we found ourselves at the crest and the rig was coasting down toward the curve, and just when we started to really get going, we stopped. Stopped dead.

The air brakes came on full with a hiss that sounded too loud. The driver sat back, shifted the controls, and took his hands off the wheel.

He stayed in the cab with his seat belt on in case all hell broke loose and he had to do something. He's not even supposed to touch the steering for this part—the hauler goes over to remote control. I can't imagine how hard it is to sit there and do nothing, or let someone else take over the lead when you've been doing the job and you haven't done anything wrong.

THING IS, BEV wasn't willing to let it go. I wondered if, with the kids gone, I'd become the focal point, the ant destined to burn under the magnifying glass. With no one else to be angry at, it was like everything I did was suddenly lit by a spotlight. She was lashing out at the world, I thought, except I was the only part of the world that was within reach. I didn't make any time for her. I didn't think about what she wanted to do. I was always late getting home from work. My day is always more important than hers. It's all true, but at the same time, it isn't any different than it's ever been. The fact that we lie next to each other in bed like statues until we fall asleep isn't helping anything. Even when I want to reach out, I can't—I can't even force my hand to make the trip, even though it's only inches. The one easy comfort we've had for our entire married life—physical touch—the one thing that we could depend on through all the other crap that falls into families, and now it's run aground. I can feel her right there next to me, and it is like I can read her thoughts, and she's every bit as paralyzed as I am. I want to sit up in the dark and shout, "We're killing everything." But I don't.

"It has to change," she finally said, the first words across the breakfast table in weeks, pressed out carefully between her lips as I brought the newspaper down to half-mast to listen.

"What has to change?"

"You have to change," she said. "For my sake."

I didn't know what to say. She looked away, and after a few minutes of silence, I ended up safely back inside the tent of the newspaper. But I wasn't reading. My head was spinning. She didn't say anything else.

I came home after work, and she was gone. One of the old suitcases was gone. Her car was gone, and there was a note in the kitchen that just said, "Think about it."

"I'm listening, I'm thinking. I always am." I even said it out loud. But the kitchen stayed quiet. My newspaper had been folded in half and put into the recycling bin, just like every other day. There was a grocery list on the fridge, and when I opened the door, there was a single pork chop defrosting on a plate on the top shelf. Somehow the pork chop, sitting there alone on its plate, only made the whole thing worse.

This will pass, I thought, and until it does, I can make toast. I can cook eggs. I can be ready when she calls.

She didn't call.

SMITTY IS RIGHT out there in front of the module for the last leg, walking backwards with the remote controller for the hauler hanging on the front of him on its neck straps, driving the whole thing like he's playing a video game, even though his eyes never stop moving. His feet never stop moving either, because he can't see both sides of the haul at the same time. Smitty's the one I always pick for the controls: Smitty was the one I picked.

His fingers barely move, hardly more than twitch, but the all-wheel-drive hauler reacts right away. When it gets tight, I put Smitty out in front, and I put spotters on all the corners along with one guy who just watches the top in case anything shifts. Heck, maybe one of the street lights angles down just a little too much and, if no one notices, we hook it with a corner or something. The power company's on call in case that happens, but this company's tight with its cash. Other places, they'd send a truck out to bird-dog us the whole way.

We've been stopping every five hundred yards or so, checking the chains and the tensioners the way we're supposed to, even though I've never had one of them shift after I've checked it, before we roll again. There's only so much time to do the whole haul. I have commitments made that are going to be kept.

Two inches is a tiny amount of space, not even enough room to squeeze between the rig and the bridge railings, so the only way to get to the back is to climb over the top of the rig and make your way along the gangway that's built right into the module for when it's set up offshore and operating. I can't send anyone up there when we're rolling, so the front and back talk back and forth on walkie-talkies. I'm watching Smitty and he's got an absent-minded little smile on his face, like he was actually somewhere else and if I didn't know him so well, I would have been worried about that. It takes a lot to stop that much weight, and I made sure ahead of time there'd be no one in the dockyard until seven—no one in doing any unscheduled overtime, no watchman out for a little fresh-air stroll—because just a little nudge from all that weight and there'd be a lot more than a beer bottle falling into the yard. It would be raining concrete.

One of the new guys on the crew yells and Smitty stops right away, but it turns out to be nothing—a piece of tire retread that he thought came from one of our wheels, but that one of the spotters had seen on the side of the road from in front, and kicked away from our tires. We get going again. I'm not even looking at my watch anymore, because we've got a tight right-hand turn and a straightaway all the way to the docks even after we get through this squeeze, and I'm pretty sure rush hour's going to catch up with us before we get it there. Suddenly there's a racket and I see Smitty's hands come flying off the controls, usually unflappable Smitty, and everything stops all over again.

But this time, it's not any of my crew shouting. I look down over the side of the overpass, the rig right next to me pressed up against my side so I can feel it trembling while it sits there, waiting, like a big animal waiting for a chance to pounce.

Forty feet down and off to the right, there's a car stopped on the street with its headlights thrown out across the pavement, both of its front doors open, and there's a young woman on one side of the car and a man on the other, and the early morning air is so darned heavy and still that I can hear their voices as clearly as if they were right up there on the overpass with us.

First she yells and then he yells, back and forth, back and forth like a tennis match with words, and he calls her a bitch and she calls him an asshole. And then she calls him a "dickless wonder" and it's like that strikes a chord with him and his arm comes up, almost like it's on strings and he's cutting the distance between them, his fist making little darting motions like it first has to find the measure of the air and the physics and the distances involved. Engineering a way from his fist to the side of her face. Forty feet down and two hundred yards away.

This would be the time when it would be nice to have some of those police cars that are supposed to be escorting us, but they gave up for a nap when they saw how slow we were going to be going.

I let out a yell from all the way up on top of the overpass, it feels like a quarter of a mile away. "Hey!"

Nothing more than that, just enough to let him know that he's not all alone with her down there, that there's someone else who can see what's going on.

He hears my voice and looks up at me, his face little more than a pasty smear but turned up my way for sure. He looks up long enough for me to know that he's seen me with all that orange and blue and yellow metal piled up behind me, like I'm a circus barker for an industry freak show, and then he turns and starts walking toward her.

She's not even yelling anymore, just watching and backing up, her hands thrown out in front of her now, wrists turned—and the only sound I hear is the grumble of the engine from under the rig.

Smitty is looking at me with his hands hovering over the controls, not touching them. The crew knows not to move the thing as much as an inch without my say-so. I look at them, and I look back over the side, where the man is closing in on the woman.

I watch from the overpass, knowing that I'm the one that's going to have to go down there. That my schedule is now truly going to be shot all to hell — but screw it. And I'm going to have to run. Closer to sixty years old than to forty, and I'm going to have to run.

Me, the only one who ever gets anything done. The only one who can fix things.

That's what they just don't understand.

Then I'm yelling, "Hold on, Bev, I'm coming," and I've already got my fists up and I'm running as fast as I can.

To everyone at House of Anansi—most of all my superb editor, Janice Zawerbny, publisher Sarah MacLachlan, and the absolutely irrepressible Laura Meyer — my deep gratitude.

To my agent, Shaun Bradley, thanks again for helping to negotiate (literally and figuratively) the wilds of the Canadian publishing industry.

To our youngsters near and far, much gratitude for your patience and understanding.

Most of all, thanks to my wife, Leslie Vryenhoek, for her unswerving support and faith in my work.

RUSSELL WANGERSKY is the author of five books. Most recently, his crime thriller *Walt* was named one of the top crime books of the year by the *National Post*. Wangersky has won, or been nominated for, numerous awards for his writing, including the Scotiabank Giller Prize, the B.C. National Award for Non-Fiction, the Edna Staebler Award for Creative Non-Fiction, the Thomas Head Raddall Award for Fiction, the BMO Winterset Award, and the National Newspaper Awards. He is TC Media's Atlantic regional columnist and lives in St. John's, Newfoundland.